Reapt  ıce

ORLA
KELLY
PUBLISHING

Anne Frehill

Peace is not the absence of
war, it is a virtue, a state of
mind, a disposition of
benevolence, confidence,
justice.

Baruch Spinoza

Dedication

To the memory of three indomitable women.

My grandmother Bridget Mc Carthy nee Mulroy, who died in the prime of her life, during the 1918-1919 Flu Pandemic.

Her dear friend and relative, Margaret Conneely nee Gibbons, who subsequently reared (against all the odds) Bridget's two boys, my father James and my uncle Tom.

Last but by no means least my mother Delia Mc Carthy nee Collins, who hid for over two hours along with older children in a sheep-stack, on their way home from school, while the Black and Tans ran amok in the sleepy parish of Kilkerrin/Clonberne, Co. Galway.

Acknowledgements

I wish to express my sincere appreciation to Orla Kelly for all her hard work and, along with her designer, for the beautiful cover that encapsulates the mood of this book.

I also wish to thank all those working in the following libraries that were consulted in connection with my research on The Irish War of Independence.

The National Library of Ireland, Meath County Library, Navan, Ashbourne Library and Dunshaughlin Library.

Finally, it behoves me to mention my dear father James, who died in 2008, just shy of his 93rd birthday. James was a natural storyteller, who loved to charm his four children with tales about the wildlife which visited our farm. Hedgehogs, badgers, foxes, rabbits, hares and birds of all shapes and sizes , had all kinds of adventures as they cavorted and played in his wonderful world. Then as we grew older his stories changed to spine-tingling tales about ghosts as well as darker ones about the 1916 Rising, the Black and Tans and later the Civil War.

Prologue

(DECEMBER 1892)

The pain in her lower back is savage but she must keep on sewing.

Four whole hours bent over the frock, stitch after stitch while she completes smocking at the cuffs, neckline, and bodice. It is now just a blur of red threads, and her eyes can barely focus.

Molly takes several deep breaths while the clock on the wall ticks away the seconds loudly. Then she curses Mrs Annie Cassidy, the old widow has plenty of money, following the death of her husband a former dispensary doctor. However, she is a stickler for perfection and if every detail is not perfect, she will refuse to cough up the full fee for the garment.

Suddenly, a cramp in her stomach holds her in a vice-like grip and she clenches her fists around the table edge. Reels of thread fall to the floor and a pair of scissors go spinning across the room.

She lays her head on the table for several minutes.

The gaps between the cramps are lessening but the pain is worsening.

She knows all the signs.

The baby is coming far too early and she needs help.

When the contractions ease, she moves slowly to the door and opens it.

A rush of icy air hits her in the face.

Shivering, she peers into the inky darkness.

In the distance, a faint light glows from Burke's window.

Panic is rising in her chest.

She sets off as fast as her feet can carry her along the muddy lane.

Tears flow down her cheeks while her belly feels as if it might burst at any second.

Fear forces her to stop as an ear-piercing scream assails her ears.

Bewildered she turns her head in every direction.

On the wind comes the shrill barking of dogs from across the bog.

For some minutes she listens, while she crouches in a ditch.

Only when a second scream erupts from deep in her throat does she recognise that it is the sound of her own voice.

Then a loud popping and water gushes between her legs.

She falls backwards hitting her head on a sharp stone.

Her last thoughts are of Sarah, her little daughter, sleeping all alone in the cottage.

The seven bright stars of the Plough low in the sky, swim before her eyes and melt into a pitch blackness that engulfs her.

Contents

Chapter One

(1919)

Farmer, farmer driving cattle,
Listen to his money rattle
One-a two, three-a dollah,
Out goes he, now hear him hollah!

A stout bumblebee buzzed frantically as it tried in vain to escape. It hovered near the open sash window but at the last second it collided with the glass and dazed, it fell to the sill where it appeared to rest momentarily.

Sarah studied it's brightly coloured pile of jet black and vivid orange and the short stubby wings. On bad days, she felt like the bee, trapped in the narrow confines of village life.

Fascinated, she watched as again and again it tried to leave but failed. She knew that bees could see certain colours and that they had a heightened sense of smell but this one was damaged in some way. Sighing, she opened the window wide and the bee whizzed past her to freedom.

A cacophony of sounds from the schoolyard drifted into the classroom on that hot still day. The infant voices of the youngest pupils rose and fell in a chant-like rendition of the old nursery rhyme. Years earlier Hetty Morgan's granny had brought it back from America, having spent her youth as a nursemaid in Boston.

Now and again the Reilly twins gave whoops of delight as they wrestled the makeshift ball from Nicky Dillon. And the older girls huddled together in corners whispering about boys and the stolen kiss Katie Brannigan had with her cousin before he left for England.

Sarah finished marking the last of the copybooks and put them in a neat pile on her desk.

Then she moved to the doorway where a gentle breeze helped to cool her cheeks. The weather was hot for June and it was baking inside the one-roomed school which had 29 pupils on its roll book. Each season brought its own unique set of problems and as the schoolmistress, she had to allow for them.

Every year when the summer holidays approached the stronger boys and girls were kept at home to help save turf for the coming winter. Homework went undone and the children's concentration spans grew shorter than ever as the delightful sights and sounds of summer beckoned to them through the four long windows. She filled the last weeks of term with drawing, music, and short sketches in Irish. She was determined to ensure that they would be familiar with their native tongue. A few of the children still peppered their sentences with Irish phrases and she loved to read simple poems which Sean had penned in Irish.

It seemed to bring him into the classroom with her.

Glancing outside to check on her pupils she chewed the top of her pencil pensively. Sometimes several weeks passed without even a word from Sean as he travelled around the country from one "safe house" to another.

She was often acutely lonely and missed the large circle of friends she had in the city.

Yet, it was precisely because of his clandestine activities that she had decided to move from Dublin to Meath. It was easier for them to meet up in the byways of Meath than in the city where spies from Dublin Castle were everywhere. Being a schoolmistress placed her at the heart of the community where she could keep a close eye on all constabulary activities in the area and alert Sean.

"Miss, I have no lunch and I am hungry."

Mary Anne from first-class crept shyly into the room.

"Did you have breakfast?"

Sarah did not wait for an answer, she reached for her bag and took out four corned beef sandwiches wrapped in brown paper.

"These are for you and your little sister. Now go outside and eat them in the shade of a tree."

The child's face lit up as she ran into the yard, leading Sarah to make a mental note to bring extra food the following day.

When the church bell in the village rang to mark noon Sarah checked the clock over the mantelpiece nervously. She was on the lookout for the redoubtable Mabel Higgins from Bunbeg, who should appear on her old 'high Nellie' bicycle, at any moment if all went well.

Mabel would be dressed in a blue skirt with matching jacket and a straw boater hat. This would signal to locals that the dawn raid on the barracks in the next village had taken place without any hitches. However, if she appeared in red attire it showed that the raid had been a fiasco with possible house to house searches to follow.

The plan was that Mabel would casually greet the children playing near the school gate. Then continuing with her journey up the road past two cottages and over the hill she would fade out of sight and enter the one street which made up Somerset village.

There under the watchful eye of the local barracks, she would enter Fargan's Tobacconists and buy tobacco and a hip flask for her aged father. Then with her purchases strapped to the carrier on the back of her bicycle, she would cycle a further six miles, taking the long route home.

Suddenly, Sarah heard a loud wailing noise. Glancing outside she saw a group of children huddled together around Sally Flynn.

"Sally, stop the theatricals it's just a tiny scratch."

Then pointing to the oldest girl in the school she said.

"Mary, take Sally inside and get some ointment from the big jar in the press, use it sparingly as it will sting for a second."

The older girl nodded, "Yes, Miss."

Shaking her head in exasperation Sarah scanned the horizon for several minutes.

Then, she caught the flash of handlebars as they glinted in the sunshine and seconds later, she had a clear view of Mabel dressed in her blue jacket and matching hat peddling slowly along.

With her head bowed, she offered a silent prayer as she went back indoors to attend to her ailing pupil.

A few minutes later a smile played at her lips when she stole a quick glance out the window and caught Mabel's shadow as she disappeared around the turn in the road.

Sarah realised that the scorching heat had delayed Mabel. It was a salutary lesson, which she must pass on to Sean. He believed that his unrivalled success as Leinster Leader for the IRA's covert activities was due to his adherence to minute details. A team of close confidantes worked day and night to keep him informed of what seemed to her to be mindless trivia relating to constabulary activities at each barracks in Meath.

"Miss it's too hot outside and Kathleen Skelly is sunburned."

A red-haired boy with freckles covering his face appeared in the doorway.

Sarah smiled at the cheeky young teenager.

"Ring the bell and tell them to form a nice orderly line before they come in."

At fourteen years of age, Tommy was in his last few weeks of school and would soon be starting work as a grocer's assistant in Navan.

"Quiet! Infants put your heads down on your desks and fall asleep. The senior classes will read out the compositions I gave them last Friday for homework and the remainder of you will listen and learn."

The older children pulled faces as they trooped to the top of the room to stand beside Sarah's table.

The title "A day to Remember" gave them great scope to use their imaginations. Some dreamed of taking a train to Queenstown and then a ship to America. Others spoke of trips to the football or hurling finals in Croke Park while the girls wrote about a day in Clerys department store in Dublin. The most heart-breaking essay came from Mary Danagher, who described the day her uncle had returned from the Great War, with a wooden leg. While lanky Dan Donovan recounted the commotion at Kilmessan train station when a goods train had been derailed by the recently formed IRA (Irish Republican Army).

Sarah was aware of the incident which had taken place months earlier. Even though she tried hard to keep politics out of the classroom it invariably showed its presence in one guise or other.

At 2.50 pm she sent the children home. The heat was stifling, and she feared that one or two were about to faint. When she had locked up the school she hopped on her bicycle and rode to the first stone cottage on the left. It was just a few hundred yards from both school and village and had been the home of several schoolmasters before her.

Once inside she saw that all her books had been disturbed.

It was the same in her bedroom someone had gone through her drawers and knocked the big jam jar of spare pencils, which lay scattered across the floor.

With her heart thumping in her chest, she leaned against the iron bedpost and tried to quell the thoughts assailing her.

Has someone discovered that I am posing as a spinster schoolmistress going about my mundane life in a backwater village?

What if they have discovered that I am the wife of one of the most wanted men on the list held in Dublin Castle by the Crown forces?

Then, to her horror, she saw brown boots and the flash of distinctive plaid socks sticking out from under the bed.

Stepping a little closer, she recognised them.

"Eamon Geraghty stand up immediately, I would know those long legs anywhere."

He emerged slowly, his face red with shame. "I am so sorry Miss. I did not mean any harm."

"Then why in God's name hide in my home and snoop through my belongings?"

Sarah was trying hard to remain calm.

"And why have you not been at school for over ten days?"

"My father asked Uncle Paddy to train me as a blacksmith. He has a forge, but I hate it, the heat is hotter than hell's fire and the work is back-breaking."

Sarah remained silent but her eyes were studying his intently.

He went on. "I love books and I hope to see more of the world than just these backward villages. I read the newspapers when I get a chance."

Sarah wanted to be sure that the boy was not spying for his father.

"You are a clever pupil but that does not answer my question. Why break into my house?"

"Miss, I squeezed through the tiny window in the porch, it was unlocked. You see I decided to have a look through all your books as I wanted to prove to you and my parents that I am smart. There is more to life than this godforsaken village."

Sarah raised her eyes heavenwards.

"There was no need to creep into my house in such a manner, you almost gave me a heart attack."

Eamon sniffed loudly.

"I- know - I was wrong to come here but I honestly meant no harm. I am desperate to get out of that hell hole."

"Come down to the kitchen while I make some lemonade. We can have a chat about your predicament. Afterwards, you can help me tidy up the mess you made."

Sarah was perturbed by his unorthodox visit, but she must not reveal this to him.

She cleared her throat, she was still concerned that the boy was there under instruction from his father.

He sat at the kitchen table while she sliced lemons.

"I will be 15 next January. Pop uses the strap on us for no reason at all and he threatens to use a sharp blade on me when I try to stand up for myself. He is a barber."

Sarah bit hard on her lip she had heard stories about his father's irascibility but she had to be careful of saying too much.

"I see."

His voice sounded croaky.

"I know I was wrong to come here but I honestly meant no harm. Please forgive me and don't tell him, he will skin me alive."

She looked directly into his eyes, there was no way she could possibly know if he was sincere or merely covering his tracks now that she had caught him red-handed. She decided to play along with him for the moment.

He wiped a tear from the corner of his eye.

"Miss, you are so kind. I really did not mean to frighten you."

A plan was forming in her head whereby she could test him over time to see if he was genuine or playing the role of a disgruntled son.

"Eamonn, if you wish you can join my extra class on Wednesday evenings around seven pm. I teach higher mathematics, history, geography, and literature to other ex-pupils, who hope to try for scholarships. There will be no charge at least not now but when you secure a good job, I shall expect you to give something back so that others might benefit in a similar fashion."

There was silence for a few minutes as he looked out the window. Then his face flushed.

"Thank you so much, Miss."

She was in no doubt about his ability, he was a smart boy and could do well in several careers.

Keeping her tone business-like she added.

"As punishment for entering my house without my permission, you can tidy my garden and clean the latrine with disinfectant before you leave."

He looked puzzled. Miss, what is a latrine?"

She laughed.

"It is another name for a privy and don't look so horrified, the schoolmaster before me was good at building, it is like a proper little toilet out there with tiles and everything."

When they had quaffed the lemonade, she handed him a bucket of water and some J*eyes Fluid.*

"Now hurry up. You will be in trouble for dodging the work with your uncle, once word gets back to your father."

He shrugged

"I am always in trouble for one reason or another."

She watched him as he made his way down the garden path.

In another place, she would have visited his parents and told them about their son's unhappiness but Mel Geraghty was dangerous. Just after Christmas, she had unearthed the fact that he was a duplicitous man who carried stories to the constabulary. She would have to be careful not to cross swords directly with him.

Later, that evening when dusk was falling, she closed all the curtains and fetched her sewing box. Like her mother before her, she was adept with a sewing needle. Opening the heavily embroidered lid she removed all its contents until she reached the bottom.

She retrieved a tiny drawstring purse which contained her wedding ring and a small locket with Sean's photograph. She planted a kiss on the glass covering his face.

Then she studied his features for a moment: that magnetic smile with the lustrous eyes framed by thick bushy eyebrows.

"You are a handsome devil," she whispered.

They had been married secretly by his brother Fr. Shay less than two years earlier. Their courtship had been short as he travelled around the country constantly, rarely staying in one place for more than two nights. Yet, it was those snatched hours together coupled with the sense of danger that surrounded him that seemed to fuel their passion for each other.

Some nights when the wind howled outside and she tossed and turned in her lonely bed, small niggling doubts tormented her.

Is he really the loving, sensitive individual you see?

Or is he just a cold, calculating man who enjoys the mayhem and killing associated with the fight for freedom?

Was I so anxious to end that gnawing sense of rejection that I married in haste?

Then she would get up and write in her diary all the positive aspects about their relationship until her eyelids grew heavy and she threw herself exhausted into bed.

Her constant fear was that he would be shot dead. His activities with the IRA (Irish Republican Army) were dangerous; raids on barracks and big houses seeking arms and ammunition, as well as large cattle drives when animals were moved illegally over land disputes. She knew from first-hand experience all that could go wrong. While living in Dublin she had been an active member of the women's branch (Cumann na mban) but on moving to Meath some months earlier she had ceased activities with them.

Offering a prayer for Sean, she returned the ring and locket to their hiding place and carefully concealed the sewing box under a pile of old fabrics.

Her last act that night was one that always filled her with deep peace. She examined the night sky through a telescope that stood proudly on its mount at the foot of her bed.

When she finally lay down, she viewed that afternoon's occurrence with pragmatism.

This is a wake-up call, I must be more vigilant in future about securing my house.

She had refused to bring a gun of any kind with her to Somerset despite her training in firearms. However, Sean had secured a Webley revolver for her and she intended to request it when they got together the following week.

Chapter Two

(THREE WEEKS LATER)

"Sarah Murphy! It's so good to see you again."

"Maddie Furlong! You look so elegant, like someone who has spent months in the finest hotel in London."

The two friends embraced and then laughed at their own spontaneity. They had not met since Sarah's secret marriage.

Sarah's eyes sparkled.

"There is a hackney man waiting outside, he will carry out that heavy case for you."

Throwing her head back. Maddie took several deep breaths.

"It really is so good to be back in Ireland. Although I would not swap my life in England for a thousand guineas."

Sarah raised her eyebrows.

"Now that sounds intriguing. You must tell me every detail. Do I take it that a new man has captured your heart?"

Raising her finger to her nose in a mocking manner her friend replied.

"Curiosity kills the cat! I shall tell you all in due course."

Then observing her fellow passengers, she said.

"This station seems so tiny after the big ones in London."

Sarah grinned.

"Yes, it's small but busy and without it, I could not tolerate living in the heart of Meath. I can take a round trip to Dublin on Saturdays without any fuss. Some days I feel like I could die with boredom here in the countryside were it not for those trips."

Maddie chuckled.

"I can only imagine how you feel! I remember being shocked when I got your letter about leaving 'the big smoke' behind, but I am aware of the broader picture."

The friends exchanged a conspiratorial wink as they went outside.

Later, they sat down to a meal that Sarah cooked.

"Where did you learn to cook like a chef?"

Maddie enquired, as they feasted on the roast lamb with redcurrant jelly, baked potatoes, and cauliflower cheese.

Sarah's face lit up.

"I can thank Aunt Rita for my culinary skills, she is really a second cousin once removed but is known as my aunt and lives near Trim. Rita worked in Oyster's restaurant in Galway for years and before that in London. She is well over 60 now but still works in the local big house whenever they are entertaining important people from Dublin or England."

"Lucky you." Maddie smothered the meat with more jelly.

"She makes wedding cakes, birthday cakes, and christening cakes too for the gentry. No one would ever guess that she also keeps a safe house for Sean."

Maddie's eyes opened wide.

"How clever! So, if some of the RIC men happen to spot that she has visitors she can claim that they are ordering a cake for some Lord or other."

Sarah winked.

"Yes, she is the perfect cover for our rendezvous, an old spinster living all alone with not another house in sight!"

Maddie gasped.

"It's a perfect place for Sean to meet with you."

Sarah continued.

"All his letters are sent via Rita as I cannot risk him writing directly to me here. I cycle over every second weekend and stay for two nights I never change this pattern. It means that Sean can turn up there if he gets a chance without having to try and contact me beforehand. I just tell everyone around here that I help Rita because she has a weak back."

Maddie exhaled loudly.

"It's good I have to admit, was your cousin involved with the 1916 debacle?"

"Not in any obvious way but she always gave money to support them. She is a lovely woman, very resourceful, her physical appearance belies her stamina and youthful outlook. I think she views me as the daughter she never had and is delighted to provide a safe house where I can steal some time with my husband."

"It must be hard trying to get some time alone with him, a brave man roaming around the country - I hope your love life is not suffering."

Maddie declared with a glint in her eye.

Sarah left down her knife and fork momentarily.

"Suffice to say that it can be a feast or a famine! Some nights when we are together Sean is so tired from days of travelling that we just hold each other and sleep like little innocent cherubs but then other nights we make up for lost time!"

Maddie giggled like a young schoolgirl.

"I am glad to hear it. And what does your cousin make of your trysts?"

"I would hardly call them trysts! Don't forget that we are married but Rita is so open-minded. She told me that she had a lover for some years, a Scottish artist I believe."

Maddie edged her chair closer to the table and leaned forward.

"You are blessed to have Rita, especially while Sean is away. This is a very isolated place for someone so vibrant as you. You must have all the single men tormented with your dark, luxuriant curls and that slim, willowy figure."

Sarah poured more gravy onto her plate.

"Without Aunt Rita's safe house there would have been no point in me moving here to this isolated parish. I try to keep busy in the evenings, on Wednesdays I give extra lessons to past pupils while on Thursdays I started a group which helps distribute food and clothes to the poor."

"I am impressed." Maddie wiped the corner of her mouth with a napkin.

"We raise the money through whist drives and jumble sales and I am expected to dine regularly with the parish priest."

"You are a resourceful lady," Maddie said before she washed down the last piece of lamb with some red wine.

"I want to help all those families who are literally living on bread and potatoes, but it also allows me to hear a lot of gossip which can be useful to Sean's work."

"So, you are killing two birds with one stone."

"That's right."

Sarah went to the range and took out a steaming bread and butter pudding which she spooned into two willow patterned dishes and covered with custard. Afterwards, Maddie produced a bottle of brandy and a brightly wrapped present which she had stored at the bottom of her case.

"These are just small tokens to show how much I appreciate your friendship."

Sarah's face glowed with delight.

"Oh, Maddie! Thank you so much, that brandy is my favourite one and look at the lovely purple wrapping paper with such an elaborate bow, how beautiful it is!"

Slowly she unwrapped the present to reveal a large bottle of perfume encased in a cardboard box with the words: *Mitsouko by Guerlain.*

Maddie explained.

"It's a new perfume but it's selling like hotcakes and I think that you will love it."

Sarah removed the golden top and dabbed the liquid onto her wrists and neckline.

Immediately the room was filled with a spicy scent of cloves and cinnamon mixed with a fruity smell of peaches.

"I adore this perfume." She applied another dab behind her ears.

Maddie gave a mischievous laugh.

"You can bet that Sean will be bowled over when he meets you. I am delighted that you are so happy with him, but I know it must be difficult being on your own so much."

Sarah's eyes misted, and she wiped them with a handkerchief.

"There are many sleepless nights when I ask myself what madness possessed me to come to Meath. But I had no choice, if I stayed in the city we would never meet up as the streets are crawling with spies."

"Just be careful." Maddie looked around the room at the locked windows.

"Don't worry, I knew what I was getting into from that first day I saw Sean at the Ceili, I knew he was a rebel and a member of the volunteers."

Maddie nodded.

"You were a rebel yourself but what was it that attracted you to him?"

Sarah did not hesitate for a second.

"I had never heard such bewitching music coming from a fiddle, and then the way he held it almost as if it were some beautiful woman. At the end of his performance, he looked directly at me from under his mop of shiny hair and his eyes were dancing and full of devilment."

"You are such a romantic!"

"I know I won't deny it, I was smitten. We were sweethearts for several months but he had reservations about becoming involved with me because he was always on the move and involved in dangerous activities. Of course, I never gave up on him, even when he was in that prison camp in Wales after the failure of the rising in 1916, then as soon as he was released, we became lovers, and you know the rest of the story. He proposed and we ended up a few months later tying the knot in London with his brother as the celebrant and your good self as bridesmaid, along with that haughty but elegant woman we dragged in off the street to be our second witness."

Maddie threw her head back and laughed.

"It was such a lovely intimate ceremony, and I was struck by how handsome Sean looked, all 6 Ft 2 ins. of him in that grey suit with the striped tie. He beamed like a Cheshire cat at his beautiful bride in that ice blue dress which brought out the colour of your eyes."

"Now, who is the hopeless romantic?"

Maddie grinned.

"Yes, but it is true."

"Rita acquired that dress from Lady Amelia Barrington in Galway and then gave it to me. However, I did not tell Sean about its provenance, he is such a nationalist that he would have objected, I am sure."

"Really!"

"Yes, I took it to a good dressmaker in Dublin, who removed the original sleeves and added delicate silk ones, the dress originally came from Paris and cost an arm and a leg."

"It was stunning."

"Thanks, Rita has it in storage for me and someday I might wear it again maybe to a ball or concert if Sean can ever come out of hiding."

Sarah took a deep breath, while Maddie said.

"All in good time, you are still only 27 years old, now I must sample your perfume."

She removed the stopper from the bottle and applied a few drops to her hairline.

With the kitchen smelling like an Indian spice market Sarah opened the brandy and poured two generous measures.

"I want to hear all about your life and your shenanigans over in London. The titbits which you give me in letters only whet my appetite for more."

Pushing back tendrils of auburn hair from her face Maddie exploded into laughter.

"Where do you want me to start? My working life or my social life?"

"Firstly, I want to hear about your latest fling."

Maddie shrugged.

"Ok, here it is plain and simple. I have just had the most wonderful affair with a married man. "

Sarah gave her a look of mock horror and then added,

"A married man! How delightful!"

"We were together for about six months but sadly he has gone back to his wife in America. I knew that he was married but I could not resist his charms including his money. We wined and dined in some of the poshest restaurants in London not to mention our week-ends away in swanky hotels."

Sarah smiled.

"I love your honesty, Maddie. So, you got to see how the other half live."

"Yes, after years of nursing cranky dowagers and randy old lords in private nursing homes I finally got to experience their cossetted way of living. And it felt good being waited on hand and foot like a princess. However, I would grow bored of doing nothing after a few months, the women lead such pointless lives because they are so constrained by social convention."

"I agree but at least they don't go to bed hungry and cold like the women I see around here. No matter what they do poverty and sickness blight their lives."

Sarah's brow was furrowed.

Draining the last drops of brandy from her glass Maddie fiddled with a gold and emerald dress ring on her right hand.

"Jeff gave me this before he left. He loved me in his own inimitable fashion, but I could not reciprocate his feelings. After my disastrous marriage to Ken, I have no desire to become entangled in a long-term relationship."

"Is there any news about Ken?" Sarah's face was filled with concern.

"No. he is still in Wadsworth prison and there he shall stay, I hope, for another twenty years."

Sarah drummed her fingers on the table.

"Is he still claiming that he did not kill that poor man outside the pub?"

"Yes. He maintains his innocence, but I lived with his drunken behaviour and fits of anger long enough to know that he is capable of anything."

She shivered, while Sarah poured two more measures of brandy into the empty glasses.

"I don't want to bring it all up again but I will say that you were very brave to leave him after just eight months of marriage. I have at least two acquaintances in Dublin who insist on staying with violent husbands because they are afraid of facing the world on their own."

Maddie swallowed a couple of mouthfuls of alcohol and stared out the window.

"It was probably easier for me because we lived in London and anything goes there. I never regretted my decision and thankfully, I had left him by the time he murdered that man. It's over seven years now since I ended my farce of a marriage and it seems like a lifetime ago."

Sarah held her glass up.

"I just want to say how proud I am of you and how much I admire your courage. To the future and to our mutual happiness and health."

They clinked glasses as a tear fell from Maddie's eye.

The following day marked the last of the school year and Sarah invited her friend into the classroom to talk to the children about the world of nursing and life in London.

Maddie was reluctant at first, but Sarah used her powers of persuasion.

"Look your talk might inspire some of the girls to go to England in a few years and train as a nurse like you did. You can even tell them about your experience of nursing soldiers sent home from the war. At the least, it will let them see that there is a whole world out there apart from domestic service in a big house or being some man's chattel with pregnancy after pregnancy. It will do the boys good too as there are scant opportunities for them around here when they finish school."

In the end, Maddie spoke to them for over an hour and she was delighted to find that they had several questions for her. Before the children left Sarah gave them all small bags of boiled sweets. There were at least two seniors who would not be returning in September and she presented them with diaries.

Afterwards, when Sarah was locking up Maddie declared.

"You are a great teacher you were made for this career."

Sarah threw her hands in the air.

"Thanks for the compliment I enjoy it of course but I don't intend to spend my life teaching in some rural backwater. I want to make a difference to women's lives and I can only do so much through the classroom. Further down the road, I might do something different, but we need to get the British out of our country and learn how to self-govern before any of my dreams can materialise."

Maddie placed her hand on her friend's shoulder.

"What did you think of those pamphlets I sent you last winter?"

"They are great! When I visit the poorer women, I chat to them about basic hygiene in the kitchen and indeed personal hygiene. Since the outbreak of the Spanish Flu last year, they are willing to sit down and listen to me. In Dublin and some of the local towns, there have been several deaths caused by that variation of the flu, fortunately, Somerset seems to have escaped so far."

Maddie lit a cigarette and inhaled it slowly as a linnet sang nearby. Then her eyes assumed a faraway expression.

"Suffice it to say that the Spanish flu took thousands of lives in the greater London area. A friend, who trained with me when we were both student nurses died, and two more friends succumbed to pneumonia some weeks after being in contact with patients who had contracted the disease."

"I am so sorry." Sarah patted her friend's shoulder.

Maddie swallowed hard and then in a barely audible voice said.

"Can we please change the subject before I bawl like a child in public?"

Sarah nodded.

"You recall the book you gave me on birth control before I got married, I am happy to tell you that it has been a God-send."

Maddie gave a throaty laugh.

"I love your choice of words! I don't think that many priests of the Catholic persuasion would agree."

With a mischievous grin, Sarah continued.

"I know that nothing is 100 percent safe but at least it gives us some knowledge and a little control over our own bodies."

"Well, condoms in one form or another have been around for hundreds of years, but they are available only to the more fortunate women. So, it is important to know that there are other options. Professor Greene, who taught me a lot about gynaecology and obstetrics, believes that within the next 50 0r 60 years, there will be a pill which men or women can take to prevent conception taking place."

Sarah cleared her throat.

"My goodness what a difference that will make to so many women's lives. I hope we live to see it. My own mother died in labour like a pauper at the side of the road, my father had deserted her some months earlier. She was on her way to seek help from the family who lived nearby."

"I am so sorry to hear that she had such a horrific death. As you know, my mother too died about a year after I was born. It seems that she never recovered from the birth as she got tuberculosis when I was a few months old."

Sarah sighed.

"I think that is the reason we became such close friends from the day we started school. I can still remember bullies teasing me about having no mother or father and sneering that my granny was old. Then you told them that you lived with your granny too because your father was a sailor, and your mother was dead. So, they started shouting rhymes about drunken sailors but you hurtled back insults at the leaders of the gang."

Maddie spoke, in a voice filled with emotion.

"It was us against the world, after the first few weeks we learned to find their weak spots and give as good as we got. I suppose it made us stronger over time as we both learned to stand up for ourselves."

They had by now locked the school doors and windows and secured the two gates which led into the playground. They were just about to set off on foot for Sarah's house when a shiny grey motor car stopped with a jolt and a cloud of black smoke.

Sarah whispered into Maddie's ear.

"Here comes Mr Terence Flynn, the local publican, grocer, undertaker, and money lender. And he has his bloody eye on me as his next wife, the last one drowned. Go along with whatever lies I tell him."

Maddie winked at her as the widower emerged from the car and removed his tweed hat.

"Good afternoon Miss Murphy."

He smiled to reveal teeth that were perfectly even but yellowed from tobacco smoke.

"Good afternoon to you too Mr Flynn."

"Are you not going to introduce me to this lovely lady?" His eyes took in every inch of Maddie from her glossy hair to her fashionable red shoes.

Once the formal introductions were over, he invited them to go for a drive followed by tea in the Royal Tara hotel in Navan. Sarah declined his offer insisting that she had an appointment with parents about their son's learning difficulties.

He shrugged.

"You know, Miss Murphy some day you will grow old and when you look back you will have one big regret."

Wearing a deadpan expression Sarah said.

"And you are going to tell me what that regret will be."

"You will regret the fact that you never enjoyed yourself or had any fun! You spend every single second thinking about those pupils, you have no life of your own outside school. Big mistake! He pointed a brown stained finger in her direction.

Sarah shrugged.

"Whatever will be will be Mr Flynn. Maybe I am happy on my own have you never considered that possibility?"

He turned to Maddie.

"I hope you have more sense than Miss Murphy. Such a beautiful face and those come-to-bed eyes, wasting her charms, living the life of a nun. I could offer her a good life, trips into the city, plenty of money, she could have anything she desires."

Maddie laughed. "I live in London Mr Flynn and anything goes."

He sniffed. "I dare say it does, but this is a Catholic country. Now I must be off, good day to you both."

"Goodbye, Mr Flynn."

The women echoed in unison as he coaxed the car back into life after some groans and squeaks from the engine.

They watched him take off in a cloud of dust, narrowly missing a sheep that had strayed onto the road. When the car disappeared around a bend they broke into fits of laughter.

"The way you flicker those big eyes! No wonder he is besotted with you!" Maddie exclaimed.

"Am I a flirt? I don't care once he keeps on believing that I am just a spinster who cannot see past her teaching profession."

"Well, if he has his way you won't end up as a spinster." Sarah grinned.

"Such arrogance! He sees it as his mission in life to save me from spinsterhood. You should have heard his angry outburst last year when women got the vote for the first time. I was in his shop and I quickly pointed out that it did not mean equal voting rights for women but only for certain categories."

Maddie's eyes narrowed

"Be careful around that man! Underneath all that smarmy talk there is a steeliness! You may have to go out with him a couple of times just to keep him happy and then invent some boyfriend who has come back into your life."

Sarah quickened her step.

"Yes, money is power but for the moment let's forget about that ass and enjoy the day together. How about cycling up to Tara? There is a spare bicycle in the shed and you can use it once we pump up the tyres."

"A ride to Tara sounds magnificent, I remember learning in school that it was the seat of the High Kings of Ireland." Maddie's face shone with delight

"Yes. Daniel O Connell also held monster meetings there at the height of his career. You can see several counties on a clear day from the top of the hill. Last year I strolled there on midsummer's night with Sean, it was magical. There was heavy rainfall, so we had the place all to ourselves otherwise Sean would not have taken the risk of appearing in public."

Maddie joked.

"You brazen hussy! What would the locals say if they had seen you swanning around on the arm of a wanted man?"

Tightening the hairpins in her bun Sarah added.

"What would they say if they saw what we did in the shade of some old oak trees?"

Maddie exclaimed.

"You never risked it!"

Sarah just smiled wickedly.

On Wednesday afternoon Sarah went with Maddie to Kilmessan train station where she bid her farewell.

"I shall miss you so much, the cottage will be empty without you, all the fun we had and the cosy chats. "

"It was like the old days when we had those earnest discussions after school and thought that we could right all the wrongs in the world."

Maddie hugged her friend, then gazed into her face solemnly. "You take care, we are living in strange times."

Sarah's voice sounded strained.

"Don't worry about me! I am going to stay at my Aunt's house tomorrow. And I reckon that Sean will appear at the weekend."

A young boy with sunken eyes helped Maddie with her cases and found her a window seat in the last carriage. Sarah recognised him as one of her past pupils who had dropped out of school shortly after her arrival. She searched for loose halfpennies at the bottom of her handbag which she offered to him.

"Take them!"

With downcast eyes, he accepted and muttered.

"Thank you, Miss." Then he hurried off to find another customer.

Sarah kissed Maddie's cheek as a shrill whistle sounded from outside their window.

"Oh my God, I shall have to go all the way to Dublin with you if I don't get off now. Safe journey and keep on writing those long letters."

Minutes later she stood on the crowded platform and waved enthusiastically until the train had disappeared.

That same evening marked the end of her tutorials until the autumn term. To her surprise, all five students were there including Eamonn Geraghty. She gave them written tests in algebra and geometry as well as a composition on the ancient site of Clonmacnoise. After the others had departed, Bridie Lee, the oldest of the group at 17 years of age, went outside and returned a few minutes later with a huge bunch of flowers that she had hidden in the hedge.

In a shy voice, she said,

"Miss these are for you, to show my gratitude for all the help you have given me with my lessons. I am determined to apply for the teacher training scholarship next year and to do some study during the summer."

Sarah could hardly believe her own eyes when she saw them.

"They are absolutely beautiful, yellow roses, pretty pink peonies, sweet William, sweet pea, and proud lupins."

"I asked my big brother to pick them this morning, he is head gardener at Drumrath House."

When Sarah discovered a tiny spray of lily-of-the-valley at the back of the bouquet she exclaimed.

"Don't forget to thank your brother on my behalf. But I hope that he will not get into trouble for taking these flowers."

Bridget picked up her blotting paper from the table and folded it nervously.

"No need to worry, the Earl took his family to Scotland last week and the old dowager is almost blind. The Earl pays me to look after her, she is very unhappy except when I read newspapers or books to her."

"I am pleased to hear that you no longer spend your days on your knees scrubbing all those floors and steps," Sarah said, in a matter-of-fact tone but mentally she was making a note for Sean about the Earl's whereabouts and his domestic arrangements.

Later, she corrected the tests and was pleased to find that Eamonn had improved in mathematics. It was obvious that he had spent some time studying despite the long days at his uncle's forge. However, she could still not be sure if he was genuinely interested in learning or if he just attended her classes to spy for his father. There was an air of deceit about him, a certain flicker in his eye when she caught him off guard which she guessed could come from living with a violent father week in week out.

Exhausted after a long day, she went outside and lit up a cigarette.

She was longing to see Sean and feel his arms around her. While he was her senior by almost a decade, she often marvelled at his composure despite being a wanted man.

Suddenly, it struck her that he had packed as much into his life as a man double his age and a shiver ran down her spine as she worried about him being captured. Then, in the distance, she heard the hoot of an owl from a nearby barn and for a moment her heart thumped in her chest, but she scolded herself for being so silly. After years in the city, she was still getting used to all the sounds of the country-side and the sense of isolation that sometimes threatened to overpower her. Maddie's visit had made her realise all that she had forfeited by moving to such a wild place but now that the summer holidays stretched ahead, she planned to dramatically improve her social life.

Chapter Three

Three days later, Sarah opened her eyes sleepily and a dark outline of velvet curtains appeared before her.

For a second, she could not remember where she was. Then the masculine scent of spice and old leather hit her nostrils as she stretched out her arms and realised that this was Aunt Rita's house. Thoughts of the night which had just passed flashed through her mind.

Sean had arrived under the cover of darkness and she had prepared his favourite meal of pork, onions, and new potatoes. Aunty had insisted on staying with an old school friend in Trim so that they had the house all to themselves. And they had enjoyed wild lovemaking until dawn broke and then drifted off to sleep.

Reaching for her dressing gown she got out of bed and wrapped it around her slim, naked body. Then in bare feet, she tiptoed down the hall and stood at the open door which led into the kitchen, where Sean was seated at the oak table pouring over some maps.

For a few minutes, she gazed at him, the blue-black hair which morphed into thick curls whenever he was outside in inclement weather or during their most uninhibited lovemaking. The athletic body with broad shoulders and long slim fingers.

Suddenly, he saw her, and their eyes locked as he jumped up and wrapped his arms around her.

"My beautiful Sarah!"

For a few minutes they clung to each other and then having kissed her passionately on the lips, he looked deep into her eyes.

"I wish that every day could be like this one and that we were a normal married couple, instead of making do with a few stolen days and nights together."

Putting her finger gently on his lips her reply was soothing.

"Let us not dwell on the negative side but concentrate on enjoying every single minute which we can spend together over the next few days. At that, he lifted her off the floor and carried her back to the bedroom where his delicate kisses and sensitive touch made her desire him once again.

In the afternoon they rose, it was another scorching day and the smell of freshly cut hay drifted in through the open windows while swallows darted here and there against the cloudless blue sky.

"I see that Pat Moore has gathered extra hands to work in the hayfield across the road, how I would love to be able to help out too."

Sean sighed as he tied his shoelaces.

Sarah looked at her husband closely.

"I know how hard it must be for you to be cooped up here in such glorious weather but it's not worth running the risk, someone might recognise you. There are at least three men in that hayfield from neighbouring parishes."

"Forgive me, Sarah, I cherish this time alone with you, but the smell of the new hay reminded me of my childhood when I used to help save it on my grandfather's farm. Don't worry about me I will go for a long walk by the Boyne later once it is dusk."

"Talking of walks, I am going up the road to buy fresh milk from Maisie Dooley, who keeps two Kerry cows, milk does not last long in this heat."

She blew him a kiss before leaving the room.

They ate dinner ravenously. When the dishes were cleared away Sean spread a copy of the *Meath Chronicle* on the table and opened it on the second page. Pointing his pen at the main feature which proclaimed:

Newly appointed Resident Magistrate to sit in 5 different courthouses in Meath. He grimaced.

"Sarah, I want you to study this article carefully and then tell me all you know about William Taylor, I seem to recall you mentioning that your dear Mother worked for him some years ago."

She stared at the newspaper for a few moments as the print blurred before her eyes. Then taking a seat beside him she immersed herself in the article. For some minutes she read and reread it while Sean made fantastical shapes by blowing cigarette smoke into the air.

"It's obvious you are thunderstruck but drink this and it will help you deal with the shock," he said as he set a glass of whiskey in front of her.

In three mouthfuls it was empty, but she did not refuse when he refilled her glass.

"You know I cannot believe that Taylor of all people is back living so close to me and to add insult to injury he has now been promoted to the position of Resident Magistrate or RM as they call it."

Sean ran his fingers through his curly hair.

"These RM's are such a motley group of men, some have trained in law while others are just a law unto themselves, making it bend as they wish."

Sarah gave a bitter smile.

"He was a District Inspector with the constabulary and was based at Moretown Barracks when my mother worked as a cook cum maid for him."

"Please go on," Sean urged.

"After she married my father they moved into a rundown old cottage, it seems that she continued to do some work for Taylor right up to the time of her death. My Grandmother never said a good word about him."

Sean lit a cigarette.

"That does not fit in with the general picture that our people on the ground have painted as the reports are mostly favourable. After his service locally he was posted to County Down and about 7 years ago he was rewarded with the position of RM in Co. Antrim."

"It is unusual that he has come back to Meath again," Sarah mused.

"Any time that you mentioned him it was always with scorn. So, I would like you to tell me everything that you ever heard about him, his appointment to Meath remains a mystery."

Sarah wiped a solitary tear from her cheek

"I blamed him for my mother's death and that of her stillborn daughter."

"Oh, Sarah, you are trembling, your face has turned white."

"It's nothing! I will be fine."

She turned away, but he took her hand and kissed it softly.

"Tell me everything about Taylor?"

"It is like a nightmare and now here he is again, back to haunt me!"

Sarah's mouth curled downwards with contempt.

Sean persisted. "It will ease your mind to tell me."

"If you knew as much as I do then you too would blame him," Sarah said as she removed imaginary pieces of fluff from her cardigan.

"Then, please my darling Sarah tell me more."

"Well, as you know my maternal Granny reared me from the time of my mother's death. She told me that my father went to England in search of work once he realised that my mother was expecting a second baby. However, he had worked in the nearby castle as a groom and it makes no sense to me that he would up and leave his young wife just when she needed him most. I was about 15 months old at that time but after he left, she had to do occasional work for Taylor as well as dressmaking to pay the rent on the cottage."

"God be good to her," Sean said as he stubbed out his cigarette.

"Anyway, she went into early labour one winter's night around the eighth month and she died at the side of the road, along with her baby... as I told you before she was just going for help."

"It was a terrible death,"

Sarah nodded.

"For years I used to be angry that she did not just stay in the warmth of the cottage and try to give birth on her own."

"She did what she thought was best," Sean said after a pause.

"Now this is what puzzles me!" Sarah exclaimed.

Sean leaned forward intently.

"When I was about 12 years old Granny went shopping one morning while I stayed at home with a bad cold, something possessed me to look through some old documents which she kept stored at the top of a wardrobe. I found nothing of interest until I came across a rusty biscuit tin at the back. When I opened it, I discovered fragments of a letter."

Sean picked at his fingernail.

"What did it say?"

"It was part of a letter from District Inspector Taylor dated about two years after my mother's death and addressed to my grandmother. The contents of it have perplexed me ever since."

Sean exhaled slowly as Sarah continued.

"Taylor wrote that he had done his best to help her pay for my upkeep and he asked if she was pursuing my absent father for financial support."

For a few minutes, silence reigned as she regained her composure.

"It was an awful shock I spent a long time trying to piece it together like a jigsaw puzzle. It was so frustrating, just finding odd words and hoping to make sense of it all."

He sniffed.

"I assume your Granny had intended to destroy that letter.

"Yes. When Granny returned, she grabbed the pieces from me without a word and threw them into the fire. Then she gave me a thrashing. "

"But you always said that you adored your Granny," Sean replied, stroking her long chestnut hair.

"Yes. She was a wonderful grandmother. It was the only time that she ever laid a finger on me. Afterwards, she ordered me to my room."

"Something very strange there!" Sean pulled a face.

"After breakfast the following morning, Granny apologised. She explained that she had hidden that letter because

Taylor was a mean and spiteful man and it perturbed her that I had come across his words."

"Did she ever refer to the incident again?" Sean asked pensively.

"No. But a week later when I was helping her make a fruit cake, she cupped my chin gently in her hand and reminded me that she had made huge sacrifices for me. I wish I had broached the subject with her again, but I was just 17 when she died."

"My poor darling! What do you make of that letter now? He asked.

She looked uneasy but ventured.

"I wonder if Taylor forced himself on my poor mother after she got married. He did not have to worry if she became pregnant then because she was already a married woman and so the child would be deemed to be her husband's. Maybe, my father realised that the baby on the way was not his and so he deserted her."

Sean was taken aback.

"But you have no real proof of this it is just putting two and two together and coming up with five. I am no fan of Taylor or any other RM but be careful Sarah for your own sake."

"Well, in the letter he alluded to the fact that he had already paid money to my Granny. Why did he do that? And why did Granny feel free to ask him for more money some two years after the death of my mother?"

"There is something fishy about it all that's for sure but I am glad that you have at last shared it with me," Sean said as he kissed her on the cheek.

She smiled.

"I am glad too, all those years of keeping it to myself."

Sean's eyes scanned the newspaper.

"This newspaper portrays him as wise and generous in his dealings with the common people and suggests that he is an idealist in pursuit of lofty ideals. In fact, this is in keeping with the reports coming back to me which show him as a quixotic individual."

"It's a wonder someone has not taken a pot shot at him, not everyone will be impressed by his saintly nature."

Sarah's voice dripped with ridicule.

"You know Sarah that it is not that simple. If our aim is to achieve governance of our own country, we need to be taken seriously by both the British and our own people. As leaders, we must demonstrate that not only are we a force to be reckoned with but also that we are individuals who possess qualities such as integrity, accountability, and a moral compass."

"Of course, but my judgement about him is clouded." Sarah conceded.

"And you are entitled to be prejudiced about him," Sean spoke gently.

With a wry smile, she nodded.

"I know that the IRA cannot behave like a bunch of cowboys from the Wild West! Look at how the plain people were not in favour of the 1916 uprising until that half-wit General Maxwell ordered the execution of the 15 leaders."

Sean cleared his throat.

"Indeed, Roger Casement's murder followed, while he was the sixteenth to die, his brutal death was the final straw in changing the mind of the man in the street."

"Hung by the neck like a common criminal." Sarah shivered slightly.

Sean exclaimed.

"Some nights before I sleep the faces of those men I knew well, pass in front of me: the Pearse brothers, poor Joe Plunkett…" His voice trailed off.

Sarah stroked his soft hair.

"I know that at a personal level you are still mourning the loss of your dear friends and I can only guess how difficult it must be to wear a brave face in public all the time."

He reached for two cigarettes from a packet on the table. Then he lit one for her and one for himself, as logs shifted in the fire.

After a few minutes, he spoke in a calm voice.

"Keep an ear out for anything that is said about Taylor, but I think you will find that he has a clean slate."

"If there are any skeletons in his cupboard, I will root them out!" She assured him.

"Be careful, he has connections not to mention money."

"It makes you wonder why he returned to Meath of all places," Sarah observed.

"He had just one son, but he went down with Titanic. He drowned alongside his wife and infant daughter. Then last year Taylor's wife died following a short but horrific battle with cancer, my source says that he requested a transfer back to Meath as Belfast reminds him of all he has lost."

Sarah bit her thumbnail

"I have no sympathy for him!"

Sean flung his half-smoked cigarette into the fire.

"Only time will tell how he fares locally, Meath is a hot-bed of agitation, especially when it comes to land."

Sarah fiddled with a gold earring.

"That reminds me of Mel Geraghty. I found his young son in my house some weeks ago.

Eamonn claimed that he wanted to study my collection of books because his father forced him to leave school early. He is apprenticed to his uncle as a blacksmith but hates it. He entered my place through a tiny window."

"Do you believe him?" enquired Sean.

"To find out the truth I have allowed him to join the extra classes which I give for scholarship applicants. So far, he has not missed one evening and works hard but he has this shifty air about him which makes me uncomfortable."

"Well! Given his father's collusion with the RIC be vigilant! It may well be that the boy is genuinely scared of his father and wants to escape from his clutches by getting as much education as possible. However, that would still not prevent him from getting into his father's good books by spying on you."

Sarah tried to hide her fear by standing up suddenly.

"Don't I know that only too well? So, it means that I have decided to take you up after all on that offer of a gun, you made the last time you were here."

He blessed himself.

"Thank God! Before the week is out, I will arrange for one to be hidden in the privy at the end of your garden."

She ruefully remarked.

"Hopefully, I won't need to use it."

"I will rest better once you have a gun, I do worry about your safety." Sean ventured.

She shrugged off his concern.

"Look, I volunteered to come to Meath, and it means that I can see you more often than if I stayed in Dublin."

"Promise me that if it gets too much for you to bear that you will tell me straight away because I can arrange for you to obtain another teaching position elsewhere."

"I promise."

Then altering the sombre mood which threatened to ruin their precious time together she changed the subject

"Your fiddle is in the parlour, if I fetch it will you play a few tunes?"

He stood up straight to his full height of 6ft. and made a mock bow.

"For you my darling, anything is possible."

During the following hour, she was transported to faraway places. He warmed up by playing a variety of gipsy dances followed by popular pieces from Paganini and Strauss.

"Bravo! Bravo!"

She exclaimed as he laid down his violin and took another deep bow.

"Thank you, Sarah," he said, giving her a big smile.

Her eyes shone in the firelight.

"No wonder you won a scholarship to London to study at the Academy, it is a pity that you never finished your training."

"I have never regretted it for one moment. After all, I have more important things to do, Ireland's freedom is my priority. There will be plenty of time for music once the British leave."

She giggled like a young girl.

"Hel-lo What about us and what about starting a family! Don't you want three or four sons and even more daughters to people this lovely new country?"

He grinned.

"Don't you worry my lovely! There will be plenty of time to make babies!"

When the dreaded time arrived for Sean to leave, they held each other tightly in one final embrace. Then putting his coat over his arm, he left under the cover of the night sky.

She watched in silence for a few minutes while her eyes followed his ghostly shape as it went out through the hedge at the bottom of the garden and across the fields. If all went well, he would soon make his way along a muddy path on the banks of the Boyne river and then he would reappear at Bolger's bridge where a driver with a pony and trap would be waiting.

From there he would be conveyed on the next part of his journey until he reached Kelly's safe house near Ballivor. She imagined him arriving covered in mud from toe to waist and the select group of men who would be sitting in the dark, dragging on cigarettes, awaiting his arrival.

Going inside she shivered and put more turf on the abandoned fire in the parlour. Aunt Rita would be back in the morning and she longed to tell her the latest news. However, she knew that there was no point in going to bed as her mind was in turmoil.

She sat close to the oil lamp on the table and took out some small pieces of patchwork which she had brought from home. Then singing softly, she began stitching them together and as she sewed her mind replayed every single word that Sean had spoken about William Taylor. She was in no doubt that he was inextricably linked to her father's departure and her mother's lonely death. Following her Grandmother's passing, she had been assailed by a sense of total abandonment, but Aunt Rita had helped her get through her grief. And she had won a scholarship to teacher training and then built a career for herself. It was through the Gaelic League, that she had been introduced to Sean and their mutual love for each other, soon eclipsed everything.

Now, that Taylor had reappeared, she had to be careful not to revert to her former mindset. It struck her that sooner or later, to give closure to the matter, that she would have to confront him about his reasons for giving money to her grandmother following her mother's death.

She rummaged through a box of old photographs and found the only one she had of her parents. The faded sepia photograph showed the couple seated formally in some studio. Their serious expressions revealed nothing, but Sarah did see a resemblance between herself and her mother, especially with the large eyes and the high cheekbones. Her father's face seemed impenetrable, with a receding hairline and shaggy eyebrows. He looked aloof and impatient as if he would rather be anywhere except with his young wife who was dressed in a frock with a fussy hat. Wiping a tear from her eye she put it back into the box.

Then she poured herself a stiff drink. She despised her father for his cowardice and for shirking his responsibilities. Since her teenage years, she had survived by telling herself that like her mother he was dead because she never wanted to lay eyes on him again.

Chapter Four

The next day brought rain, not one ray of sunshine managed to penetrate the menacing clouds which hung over the golden hayfields.

Sarah could not get thoughts of William Taylor or her absent father out of her mind. She tried to keep busy by making two dozen pots of jam from gooseberries which she picked hurriedly in the garden between thundery showers.

It was late evening when Aunt Rita returned by hackney.

"My goodness, you have been a busy bee making all that jam! You should have waited until I came home, there is nothing more boring than topping and tailing bowls of gooseberries."

She studied Sarah who shrugged her shoulders.

"I will give the surplus ones to the poor when I do my rounds on Wednesday night. It will go nicely with bread."

Aunt Rita stood with her back to the fire while Sarah measured out two teaspoonfuls of tea leaves into a blue teapot and poured boiling water over them.

"Sarah, you look as if you have the troubles of the world on your shoulders. Has something happened between you and Sean that I should know about?"

Silence hung over the room while Sarah cut thick slices from a large quarter of fresh bread.

"No. Don't worry it's nothing like that. Did you know that there has been a new RM appointed to this district and it happens to be Taylor?"

Aunt Rita took her place at the table.

"Do you mean DI William Taylor?

"Yes, the same man who has reappeared under a different title."

Rita smoothed the wrinkles in the tablecloth with her right hand.

"You will have to tell me more."

"He is here now living in Meath right under my nose. It has brought back my poor mother's death all over again."

"Try to let it go. We are not meant to live in the past," Rita said anxiously.

"I know but it makes me wonder what part Taylor played in my Father's desertion of us.

I have always hated him, he abandoned my mother and cut all ties with me."

Rita sniffed.

"Men are a different breed than women. And I am sure now that if Thomas saw you, he would regret walking out on you and Molly."

Sarah gave a deep throaty laugh.

"Thomas Murphy never cared about anyone but himself. To add insult to injury when I wrote to his brother

Frankie soon after Granny died, he informed me that he had a large family of his own and could not help me."

Aunt Rita locked her ankles defensively under the table as she responded.

"That Murphy clan are snobbish, I can recall your granny telling me that she never liked any of them. Apparently, they did not approve of your parent's marriage because they are some jumped-up Tipperary family and they felt that he could have done better. I believe that your father is still in America, you know he went there when your mother died."

Sarah chose a chair directly opposite her aunt.

"He is some father! Imagine that he never wrote one letter to me down all those years or contributed one penny towards my upkeep!"

In a tremulous voice, Aunt Rita answered.

"It is your father's loss that he has not known you, he has missed out on so much. And I am sorry that Taylor is living in the next parish and that you have to go through all this again."

Sarah smirked.

"Thomas Murphy has no interest in me. Years ago, Granny made enquiries from neighbours who went to Boston. It seems he remarried soon after he was widowed and at last count had seven children."

Aunt Rita fixed her eyes on her.

"My dear girl there is no point in dwelling on all of this, you don't want to end up as a bitter old lady. You are such a lovely, intelligent young woman and you have a gorgeous, brave husband. Be thankful for all of that."

Sarah poured tea into two teacups adorned with pretty, pink flowers.

"I am sorry for troubling you again with this problem as you have been so kind and generous to me."

Aunt Rita leaned across the table and patted her hand.

"Life makes no sense and yet we have to carry on. Be careful with William Taylor he now has more power than ever and given that you and Sean have a lot to hide he could prove to be a dangerous man indeed. "

Sarah faked a smile.

"I know you are speaking the truth, but I have had a shock and it will take me some time to get used to the idea of seeing him around the area. Now, you will be glad to hear that I am planning a few weeks holiday, it will be a break from all of this."

"That's the best news I've heard in weeks."

Aunt Rita stretched her arm across towards the jar of jam.

"Let me sample some of this tasty jam with your bread and I will tell you all about my time with my friend Connie."

It was a week later, just after tea when Sarah cycled to the parochial house, a large, ivy-clad one at the far end of the village. The housekeeper, Miss Hayes ran it on martinet principles. Muttering to herself because Sarah had arrived without an appointment, she led her silently to a gloomy parlour at the rear of the house.

"I am afraid you may be waiting a long time Fr. Daly has an important visitor in his study. Perhaps you could come back another day."

Sarah could not resist giving her an equally caustic response.

"Miss Hayes while you may not rate me as a woman of any importance, I am in charge of the school and given that it is a Catholic school in the Diocese of Meath I need to consult with the Parish Priest about various matters. So, I shall sit it out until he is free."

She showed Sarah into a small room at the side and swept haughtily out of the room while Sarah studied her surroundings. A grim painting over the empty fireplace of some unknown saint in the throes of satanic temptation and on the wall opposite, a faded painting of the Bishop of Meath. Then her eye saw a recent copy of the Freeman's Journal lying on the settee in the corner and she settled down to read it.

In glowing language, it described Sinn Fein's leader Eamonn De Valera and his popularity at home and across America. She had met him a couple of times with Sean, but she had not been impressed by his gangling appearance and dry, mathematical approach to problem solving.

When Fr. Daly finally appeared, he was smiling.

"Miss Murphy, my apologies for keeping you waiting in such a gloomy room on a summer's evening. The new magistrate kindly paid me a visit and if you look through the curtains you may see him, a most avuncular man I would say."

She sprang to her feet and caught a glimpse of his smart hat and finely-tailored suit as he was helped into a motor car by his chauffeur.

"Why don't we have a walk in the garden and then my housekeeper can bring us something to drink."

Sarah smiled warmly as she extended a hand to Fr. Daly. He had a kind, compassionate nature but tended to take the responsibilities of being a parish priest too seriously.

"I would love to take a walk in your garden it is always a delight to behold your beautiful collection of tea roses."

He nodded his head enthusiastically, as she followed him outside.

"Well, gardening is what keeps me sane. My parish has many problems and as you well know, poverty is only one of them."

"Indeed."

For a while, they lapsed into silence as she bent to examine this rose and that or to inhale the scent of some bright pink climbers which had tenaciously wound their way around the ancient apple trees.

Later, while they sipped sweet sherry she told him about her plans to take a long holiday.

"I am glad to hear it, you work so hard not just in your capacity as a teacher but all that charitable work as well."

"It's just a drop in the ocean, I am not the kind of person who can turn a blind eye especially when I see innocent children in front of me every day who have come to school with empty stomachs."

"I wish to God we could do more for them," he said sadly.

"Talking of school, I want to tell you that I will have nine pupils for First Holy Communion at Christmas and six for Confirmation in the Spring. "

"How come the numbers of First Communicants are up this year?"

She smiled. "I have two sets of twins, the Ryan's and the Price's."

"Oh, I had forgotten. Now, one last question before we leave school business aside for the summer. How many children are enrolled for infants in September?"

"Well, about three at the moment but by the start of term that will increase as parents face the prospect of keeping children occupied over the dismal days of winter."

"Of course, on a different matter altogether, the Resident Magistrate is now the new tenant of the former Glebe house. Apparently, he ran out of his official residence two weeks ago. He claims it was damp and rat-infested and not fit for human habitation."

"That's preposterous. It seems to be in good condition, at least on the outside and I heard that there was a big restoration job done on it some years ago."

Sarah's face had turned bright red, but she managed to keep her voice steady.

He hesitated for a moment and then in a conspiratorial voice said.

"Rumour has it that he is of a nervous disposition. In recent times he lost all the members of his family. I think the loneliness of the place and the proximity of Trebinn graveyard unsettled his mind. He claims to have witnessed paranormal activity there."

Then giving a mischievous wink he added.

"I believe what he really saw was a group of IRA lads hoping to bury stolen ammunition in one of the old tombs."

"Did he have the cemetery checked out?" Sarah enquired in a matter-of-fact tone.

Fr. Daly chuckled.

"Yes, they found nothing, but it scared the magistrate as his two servants backed him up and swore they saw otherworldly activities too. So, he has had six or seven rooms made habitable in this new abode and there he is planning to stay."

Sarah forced a smile. "Let's hope that he does not hear noises in the night there!"

Then removing a bunch of large keys from her bag she left them on the table.

"All the keys to the school are here including the spare ones, there is no point in leaving them at my house. Although Aunt Rita will check on my place regularly."

"That's fine, shall I pour you another glass of sherry?" He enquired.

"No, thank you. I must hurry home. I have all my packing to do tonight as I am taking the early train at 7. 35 am."

"I do hope that you enjoy your holiday. And may God bless you. I am sure that you will be glad to get back to the city for a while."

He laughed at his own joke as he followed her down the long passageway and out into the warm evening air.

"Miss Murphy…"

She turned towards him and he clasped her hand tightly.

"A certain gentleman spoke to me recently. He is rather upset that you will not even consider spending some time with him, an evening at the theatre in Dublin or a fine meal in Jammett's restaurant."

Apoplectic with rage she snatched her hand away.

"How dare Terence Flynn talk about me in that way to you!"

"Forgive me, Miss Murphy - I did not intend to upset you. The person in question is a decent, hard-working man. He has plenty of money and I believe that any woman would be fortunate to have him as her husband."

Sarah demurred.

"He is a dandy, not to mention the fact that he views all women as his playthings. I for one have no interest in the prospect of ever being his wife."

A look of horror crossed Fr. Daly's face.

"You are too hard on him, Miss Murphy. Judge not and thou shall not be judged!"

"When did you become the local matchmaker?"

She enquired as she raised her eyes, and they met his.

"Look here Miss Murphy I mean no harm. That little house of yours must be a desolate place on long winter nights, I thought that some male company might be just what you need."

"Humph! Allow me to tell you that I do not need the presence of some man to make me happy. I have my books and other hobbies to fill those nights when I am not involved in charity work or taking part in card games."

Looking at her indignantly, he said, "I bid you good evening and a safe journey tomorrow." Then he withdrew.

"Thank you, Fr. Daly. And a good evening to you too."

Then she hurried down the garden path to her bicycle which she had left at the front gate.

Cycling home at a furious speed she almost collided with a gaggle of geese who were crossing the road.

Later, having uncovered the handgun from the privy in her garden where Sean's ally had concealed it, she carried it into the house. Then hiding it among underwear at the bottom of her brown suitcase she berated herself for showing her anger to the priest. She needed to keep him on side not only because he wielded a lot of power over her position as schoolmistress but also because half the population of the parish for several miles around viewed him as some sort of demi-God.

Sean's advice when she first moved to the area rang in her ears.

"Cross the P.P. at your peril, he has been ruling over his flock for the past twenty years and their loyalty to him knows no bounds."

So far, Fr. Daly was happy to take a back seat and allow her to make most of the decisions about the school. She reasoned that he would not see anything wrong about trying to match a lonely, spinsterish schoolteacher with a local man of property.

Shivering, despite the humidity of the early July night she piled the last of her clothes into the case and snapped it shut. While Fr. Daly had accepted that Home Rule had failed, he was still getting used to the idea that an armed conflict was required. So, he would be furious if he discovered that her whole persona was false. Add to this the fact that she was married to one of the most wanted men on the whole island and there was no knowing what he might do. She knew that his only priority would be his flock and that he would view her as endangering them by her clandestine activities. She resolved once she had settled in Bray to post him a watercolour which she would paint of a seascape. Along with it she could send him her best wishes and add that on reflection she had come to realise that she had over-reacted to his kind and paternal interest in her well-being.

Before settling down to sleep that night, she decided to take a final stroll through the back garden and witness the beauty of the dew on the flowers. She stooped to pluck a half-closed rosebud from a small bush.

"Ouch, you got me with your prickles!"

She shrieked, as tiny drops of blood oozed from her finger. It was then that her ear caught a muffled crackling sound from the corner where there was a large group of bushes. Stemming the flow of blood by putting her finger into her mouth she hurried down the path expecting to discover a set of badgers or a nest of hedgehogs. Instead, she saw through a gap the outline of a male running as if his life depended on it across the hayfield.

Screwing up her eyes tightly she tried to focus but his form seemed to weave in and out between haycocks until he merged into the shadows in the fading light. Her heart felt as if it could jump out of her chest and she hurried back indoors to bolt the doors and windows.

Hoping to compose herself she made a hot punch. Then she started to draw the rosebud which had pricked her earlier.

After a few minutes, she abandoned the task.

It was difficult to draw well in the flickering lamplight.

And her mind was working feverishly, trying to unlock the identity of the prowler.

He could be some peeping tom or even a past pupil.

Or was his mission a more ominous one?

Was he sent to spy on me by someone who knows I am hiding something?

It was well past midnight when she finally went to bed. She was looking forward to spending a few days with acquaintances in the city before going on to Bray.

And at the end of the month, she had arranged to take a long weekend with Sean at a remote beauty spot in Wicklow.

She closed her eyes and sighed. In just a few hours she would be getting away from the constant scrutiny of locals. It was the price to be paid for being the schoolmistress in a small village like Somerset.

Chapter Five

"Miss, would you mind letting Johnny have the window seat?"

Sarah looked up from her book into the eyes of a heavily pregnant mother, who was wiping her young son's snotty nose with a filthy handkerchief.

"Miss, this is his first time on a train."

The little boy put his head down and peered at Sarah under his eyelashes.

Sarah winked at the child

"No, of course, he must have it, just allow me to gather up all my belongings."

A few minutes later she took an aisle seat further on in the carriage and relaxed. She could hardly believe that the holidays were over, she was on her way back to Somerset after six delightful weeks. Closing her eyes, she allowed her mind to wander as the train screeched and shuddered as it left the station behind. It would take at least an hour and a half before reaching her destination and if cattle strayed onto the line a lot longer.

She had enjoyed a couple of weeks at Price's Hotel near the city centre, meeting with friends and catching up with various acquaintances.

Then, in August, she had moved to Bray where she found a small boarding house just off the promenade. Taking a long walk every morning along the seafront with magnificent views of Bray Head and the Sugarloaf.

Finally, her last glorious week was spent with Sean in the Wicklow mountains, where he could let down his guard. Hiking by day and camping under the stars at night, they did not stand out from the handful of other couples enjoying the outdoors, with their sunburned faces and aching limbs.

"Apples, sweets or holy pictures?" Sarah jumped with fright as she opened her eyes to see a bedraggled woman standing beside her.

"I will take a bag of sweets."

She said, taking some coins from her pocket. Then placing them in the woman's hand she added.

"Keep the change."

"May God be good to you."

The woman grinned to reveal rotting front teeth and then fished out a paper bag from her frayed basket.

Sarah had no intention of eating any of the sweets, she knew from experience that the poorest of the poor had all kinds of tricks for making a simple bag of sweets go further than normal as they needed every halfpenny. Watching her make her way through the carriage Sarah felt enveloped by sadness. The woman reminded her of her own mother and how she must have struggled to make ends meet once her father abandoned them. And once again it raised the question of why Taylor had helped her grandmother.

Looking out the window she tried to distract her mind by watching the landscape flash by.

it was another lovely day, and the fields and little villages were bathed in a golden light. Turning to the elderly man who was seated beside her she asked.

"Would you mind if I leaned across and opened the window?"

"Do what you like," he answered grumpily and returned to his newspaper.

Once the window was lowered, she inhaled the balmy, sweet air that smelt of saved hay and wildflowers. And as her eyes followed the sparkling surface of a small river winding its way through grassy banks with clusters of trees at the side, she was aware of nothing but the beauty of nature.

The following morning, Aunt Rita, who had arranged to stay with her for a short break, arrived. They spent the entire day preparing the schoolhouse for the reopening on the first of September. Just as Sarah was locking up, she noticed a figure on a bicycle peddling furiously in her direction.

"Miss Murphy, Miss Murphy!"

It was only then that she recognised her as Mrs Geraghty, the barber's wife. Nodding to her aunt that she could go on home she waited nervously while Lizzie dismounted.

"What can I do for you on this glorious evening?" Sarah enquired as she sat on the stone wall in front of the school and invited the woman to join her.

"Can we go around to the back because I don't want my husband to see me talking to you?"

Sarah tried to make light of the situation as she answered.

"I am hardly the enemy but follow me, we can go inside if it makes you feel happier."

Once they were seated indoors at a long desk, the woman took several deep breaths and after a few minutes managed to splutter.

"Woe betide anyone who crosses my man."

Sarah went to a press behind her table and found a small bottle of Powers which she kept hidden for Fr. Daly, who liked to have a shot of his favourite whiskey whenever he visited the school. Pouring a generous amount into a cup she handed it to the distressed woman.

"Get this into you first, it will help you. And then you can tell me everything."

Sarah waited while the hands of the wall clock headed for six.

"It's all about Eamonn and the fact that he hates working in his uncle's forge. The big man is determined to make a blacksmith out of him."

"Do you mean your husband Mel?" Sarah interjected.

Lizzie finished the contents of the cup.

"That's right. He is determined to stop Eamonn from going back to your evening classes, he says that you are filling the boy's head with all sorts of nonsense and that you should be reported."

"Reported? When all I am trying to do is improve the boy's opportunities. Look here, please be aware that Eamonn approached me about extra tuition, not the other way around. I have plenty of past pupils who are happy to avail of free classes."

"I know that is all true, but will you promise to stop instructing him?"

Sarah heard the panic in the woman's voice and noticed the way she tapped her right heel repeatedly on the wooden floor.

"I have no desire to cause any conflict in your home so rest assured that if Eamonn turns up for class next week I will tell him about this conversation."

Lizzie lowered her voice.

"I have something else to say to you before I go… I am telling you to your face as I like you …. but if Mel thinks that you are encouraging Eamonn to turn against him…"

Sarah met her eye unflinchingly.

"I am not aiding and abetting your son …. if you don't want your son to receive my tuition that is fine by me. Is there anything else you want to tell me?"

She whispered.

"Mel likes to get his way…and don't say that I did not warn you as he thinks that all women should know their place…."

Sarah watched in astonishment as she hurried out of the room.

Then she took a few swigs of whiskey from the bottle before putting it back in its hiding place. Sometimes she asked herself why she did not just stick to the main school hours like many teachers she had encountered. However, she knew the answer was simple, she did not want her past pupils to struggle to make ends meet like her mother and so she tried to equip them with extra knowledge which would give them a better chance in the workplace.

After a cold supper which Rita had waiting for her, they retired to the tiny mock ruin which the previous incumbent had begun to build with his own hands but never managed to finish. On a summer's evening, it was a place of stillness with only the first gleam of moonlight stealing through the gaps in the red bricks.

For a while, they sat in silence.

Then Rita exploded.

"I cannot get over the cheek of that woman! After all, you are only trying to give her son a leg up in the world."

"Don't worry about her Rita, it is the old viper hiding behind her that I need to watch."

Rita removed her spectacles and cleaned them with a blue handkerchief, then placing them at the end of her nose she peered at Sarah.

"I am not worried about that pathetic woman, but I am worried about you. Juggling teaching, unpaid tuition, and charity work and then there is Sean moving from one place to another under the cover of darkness."

"Yes. I get the picture, but I am not going to do anything rash. I promise you that I will not give young Eamonn any more tuition as I certainly don't wish to step on his father's toes. He has passed me by in the street a couple of times and if looks could kill I would be dead by now."

Crossing her arms tightly Rita said.

"I am so relieved. Now just to tell you that Mary Moore from Crosshill works as a charwoman for the new RM … I know her sister, it seems that he spends his weekends drinking … he has given Mary all the gory details about the deaths of his son and family on Titanic and then the cancer which took his wife."

"It's seven years since Titanic sank so he must be in a bad way when he is talking to a charwoman in such a manner," Sarah said with derision.

"Mary Moore seems to think that the demon drink will kill him, but time will tell. Now I must hear more about your holidays, those weekly postcards were much appreciated but I want all the news." Rita's eyes shone mischievously.

On the first day of the new term in keeping with tradition Fr. Daly visited the school and offered prayers for the year ahead. Much to Sarah's dismay her would-be suitor Terence Flynn stood by, watching the proceedings through the window. Just as the priest was giving an individual blessing to the innocent young faces lined up in front of him Terence Flynn slipped quietly into the schoolroom and waited at the back.

Although she was busy comforting the infants on their first day away from home she noticed his amused expression and felt like throttling him.

"Now, I must hurry I have to make a sick call to old Mrs Keogan, I am told that she is in her final agony," The distracted priest declared.

"I am sorry to interrupt but I have a plan to help your pupils."

Flynn's voice seemed to boom off the walls as he strode to the top of the class.

"I cannot spare another minute Mr Flynn, but you can share your ideas with Miss Murphy here and we can all meet up in the parochial house later in the week. Now, children do try to be good for your teacher and remember that your schooldays are the best days of your life."

Mary-Kate Cassidy rushed to open the door for him while Sarah and her suitor both replied. "Thank you, Fr. Daly."

Then Sarah immediately took charge of the situation, in a stern tone she said.

"Mr Flynn I have a lot of work to get through this morning, so I suggest that you go home and write down your proposal and we can convene later in the week as suggested."

"For heaven's sake, I came here to talk it through with you not to be dismissed like some bold schoolboy!"

He looked directly into her face as a waft of his breath heavy with tobacco hit her. "

Aware that the older pupils were hanging on every word she addressed them.

"Children I want you all to take out your copybooks and draw some fruit, maybe an orange or an apple."

Amidst the rustle of pages and the whisperings of the children, she spoke with an air of contrived calmness.

"Mr Flynn in one sentence please tell me your suggestion then I must insist that you leave, these children need to get on with their lessons and I need to teach them."

"That's what I love about you, always so conscientious and so concerned about your little charges," he said sotto voce.

"Mr Flynn my patience is wearing thin."

"Okay, I want to set up a prize in my late wife's name, maybe I could pay for one of your pupils to go on to secondary school for a minimum of three years."

Sarah's chest felt as if it might explode.

"There is no doubt about it any donations would be welcome but to avoid jealousy among neighbours, prizes need to be carefully managed."

He beamed.

"I am so glad that you approve."

"Thank you for your offer which we will discuss along with Fr. Daly on Tuesday night at 8 pm. Now, you really must go," she said doggedly.

Taking her hand in his he held it tightly.

"Thank you for your time, Miss Murphy, I shall look forward to that meeting."

Withdrawing her fingers from his sweaty grasp she answered.

"I was involved in a similar scheme in a Dublin school a few years ago so I know the pitfalls but we can work out something."

Purposefully, she walked to the door and opened it for him. Then raising her eyes to meet his as he departed, he winked boldly at her while she banged the door loudly in his wake. Deep in her heart she knew that he had just laid a snare for her, he had no interest in her pupils, but it was his devious way of buying time in her company.

The early September evening was cool and damp as Sarah cycled to the parochial house for the meeting. She found that Terence Flynn had ensconced himself in the front parlour with a full glass of whiskey while the priest was pouring over a large ledger.

"Ah! Now we can get down to business!" He said with a grin in her direction.

Fr. Daly pulled out a mahogany chair for Sarah near the table and then in an officious voice spoke.

"So, the purpose of this meeting is to discuss how we can utilise Mr Flynn's generous offer. Miss Murphy, may we have your opinion?"

"Mr Flynn, I believe that it would be impossible to set up a prize as you suggested. For a start I have only three pupils who will finish national school in June, one has great learning difficulties and cannot read or write so that means that we would be pitching the remaining two against each other. They are both smart children, who work hard. Therefore, I think it would be grossly unfair to do so. Now if there were more pupils in that class it might be possible to implement such a prize but, in this case, the loser and their family would be left embittered."

"Patience is a virtue and I have plenty of it, Miss Murphy. I shall be guided by your experience as I do not claim to know much about education."

The priest twirled the top of a fat fountain pen on the table.

"I agree with you, Miss Murphy."

Then turning to Terence Flynn, he said.

"But we are not turning down your offer Mr Flynn."

A pause ensued, then the priest continued.

"Perhaps, you might consider my suggestion which is that you commemorate your late wife by paying for the cost of new windows in the school, God knows they are long overdue.

We could erect a plaque in her memory and if you wish you could donate money towards new schoolbooks, wall charts and so on for the benefit of all the pupils. We are all Catholics here Mr Flynn and we do not wish to do anything that would prove to be divisive."

Under the table, Sarah's hands were clenched tightly, and she forced herself to nod in agreement with the priest while they awaited a response.

Flynn twisted his mouth as he looked from one to another, savouring the moment as silence engulfed the room. Then swallowing his whiskey in one go, he hit the table for effect with his fist and with eyes flitting from one to another he declared.

"I believe we have a deal. Fr. Daly feel free to go ahead and send the glazer's bill to me. Miss Murphy can you research how much it will cost to buy new schoolbooks as well as modern equipment for the classroom and I will give you a cheque."

"Thank you, Mr Flynn. You are most generous, and we can talk more about a nice brass plaque in memory of your dear wife once the work is completed.

The priest's eyebrows contracted as he wrote notes in a small black diary.

"Yes. Thank you, Mr Flynn. Please allow me to assure you that every single pupil will benefit from your philanthropy."

Her throat felt dry, but she had to be seen to acknowledge his generosity.

"Come, Come, don't we all know each other too well for any mistrust? Indeed, Miss Murphy, I know that given your scrupulous nature, not one penny will be wasted."

Sarah forced a quick smile in his direction but inwardly she was seething that he always managed to revert to the stunted image he had of her.

"So, I can bring this meeting to an end."

Fr. Daly stopped writing and rubbed his eyes for a few moments. Then he smiled broadly, to reveal several yellow teeth.

"And thank you again, Mr Flynn, especially for your readiness to agree with my suggestions. The important matter here is that you wish to mark your darling wife's short life and untimely death and I know that we have just decided on the most fitting means of doing so."

"Indeed," replied Flynn as his eyes darted in the direction of Sarah who was staring out the window.

The next evening Sarah watched with a sense of unease while teenage boys and girls arrived at her cottage for the evening class. When the church bells from the village chimed six, she settled the group around the big table in the kitchen and began to parse some Latin sentences. And just at that moment, Eamonn Geraghty entered the room, she had been so absorbed in her work that she had not heard his light knock. He nodded in her direction and bowed his head, as he spoke.

"Miss Murphy I am sorry for being late and disturbing the class."

Sarah felt dizzy as she took in the pallor of his face but rising to her feet quickly, she took control.

"Please continue with this work while I have a word in private with Eamonn."

She beckoned to him to follow her into the sun-filled back garden. Once they were out of view of the kitchen she spoke in a smooth voice.

"Eamonn you have a natural quickness of mind and a great imagination and I hope that you will in time be able to pursue your own career path. However, your parents are adamant that I cease giving you any more lessons."

He kicked a tuft of grass with his heel.

"They have no right to stop me from learning I want to continue studying with you, don't take any notice of them. I bet Da sent Ma over here last week to put an end to my dreams."

"Let me finish. Your mother insisted that I give an undertaking that I would not allow you to attend my evening classes. I am so sorry, but I have no choice, you are still a minor and I cannot go against them."

"Curse them both! I hate them and someday they will live to regret this. Miss Murphy, I am disappointed as I thought that you were different, but I realise that you are like all the others. You are terrified of that devil they call my father."

He threw his books into a rose bed and then muttered to himself.

Her heart was heavy with sorrow for his predicament, but a plan was forming in her head. "Let me counsel you for a minute, you must stop attending these evening classes but there is nothing to prevent you from continuing with your studies on your own."

The boy opened and closed his fist and then spoke.

"What do you mean?"

"I cannot be involved any further, but I can loan you some books. If you give me a few days I will pick out some in mathematics, Latin and Geography. And I shall do out a whole copy full of exercises, complete with guidelines and tips for you. Do not come back here again but if you check the big oak tree near Teehan's well on Saturday evening you will find them hidden there."

"Yes, yes, thank you so much," he said as his face brightened and he stooped to retrieve his books from among the thorny bushes.

"Now go and good luck to you."

She watched as he walked around the side of the cottage and down the path to the front gate. Then, without a backward glance, he sped off down the road, on his bike.

Silently she offered a prayer for him.

For a moment she felt guilty about dismissing him from her evening class.

Yet she did not dare risk drawing the wrath of his father upon herself.

She had to calm her inner turmoil by counting to 20, before returning to the other students, working assiduously at the translation of a Latin poem.

Chapter Six

Six busy weeks had passed since the start of the school year. The night was stormy, gale force winds rattled the galvanised roof on Rita's old garden shed with alarming ferocity.

"That roof will be wrenched off before the night is through," Sean observed. "And I am wondering if I should go out and try to secure it before the worst happens."

"Please do not go outside into the eye of the storm! Although we are minding Rita's place while she is in Cork, she would not expect you to risk life and limb."

Sean laughed.

"Ok, I get the message! Can I blame you when she comes back and sees just a pile of timber in place of her shed?"

They were sitting together on a settee in front of a roaring log fire and she leaned closer to kiss his cheek.

"Thanks to the storm you cannot leave tonight so I am getting extra time with you."

"Sarah, you are a hopeless romantic, but I have to admit that I am not complaining about the extra time together."

He raised his heavy black eyebrows until they reminded her of caterpillars.

"I would love to keep you here all to myself."

"I will leave at first light, if Patsey Casey is not waiting for me at Geeren, I can slip through the bog and head for Kells, I should reach old Ma Duggan's by nightfall."

Stroking his hair back from his forehead she gave a thin smile.

"Stay safe! I worry when you don't reply to my letters immediately."

Sitting up straight he studied her eyes.

"We have been through this before I am a wanted man and I often have to lie low for days…. don't forget that I too worry…. about your safety."

"Do you think that I can't take care of myself?"

She enquired with an air of mock indignation.

He hesitated for a few seconds and then explained.

"That last letter from you was upsetting when I read how Lizzie Geraghty threatened you and you helping their son."

Sarah's neck stiffened. "I don't expect to hear from them again as I have done as they requested and dropped Eamonn from the evening class. Besides, I was told about another ugly episode involving him on my way here."

Sean frowned. "What is he up to now?"

"This is about an incident last week when someone attacked him on his way home from Deegan's pub."

"Is the word spreading that he is telling tales to the constables?" Sean exclaimed.

"It seems that he has been aiding and abetting his cousins to steal cattle and sheep but the powers that be are turning a blind eye to it all."

Sean shrugged. "Geraghty is duplicitous, he keeps in with the clergy by making donations towards educating young men for the priesthood in Maynooth. And he has been known to be generous to poor widows."

Sarah gasped. "So, that's how he survives. But if he is killed won't the top brass in the RIC just find someone else to replace him?"

"Indeed. But I think that Geraghty will continue to prosper for the present at any rate."

"So, your counsel is that the devil you know is better than the one you don't know."

Sarah's eyes twinkled as he took her hand and kissed it. Then he exclaimed.

"We have the measure of him. Let the hare sit!"

"Fair enough! Now, I want to tell you that I have quenched that flame Terence Flynn had for me."

He thumped the armrest. "Tell me all."

"His money has made a huge improvement in the lives of my pupils. He delivered on all his promises, new windows, new textbooks, and all the latest aids for the classroom."

"Look here, don't feel guilty about it, he is loaded!" Sean pulled a face.

"Oh yes, I know. To show our appreciation we had the unveiling of a plaque in memory of his late wife at the school last Friday. Fr. Daly invited all the pillars of the community along with a reporter from the *Meath Chronicle*, so Flynn got his few minutes of fame."

"And the brats got a half-day off from school," Sean added, with a smile.

Sarah gave him a playful slap on the arm.

"Listen it's no joke. That same evening there was a formal dinner for him at the Parochial House and I was invited. Of course, I was seated next to him and after the pudding when the other guests moved to the parlour, I put him out of his misery."

"I am glad, it's not fair to string a man along even a wealthy one." Sean winked.

"I told him that during my summer holidays I met a doctor from Bray who works in London and that we exchange letters every week. Then I added a few glowing comments about his work with the poor and the elderly there."

"Did he take the hint?" Sean said as he fiddled with his pocket watch.

"Yes, he got the message as I added jokingly that now he won't have to worry about me wasting away into an old embittered spinster."

"How did he respond to that?"

"OK. He wished me well and then he excused himself and joined the men in the other room. Miss Hourican and Miss Ball, who help with our annual fund-raising events, were seated at the head of the table. They heard every word and their eyes nearly fell out of their heads at this latest gossip."

"Great. That means the word will spread that you have a sweetheart in London and so you will not have to deal with more unwanted attention from lonely males."

She kissed him lightly on the lips.

"That's the plan anyway."

He stood up and stretched his long limbs.

"Well, Mrs Byrne I have my own plans for you!"

Lifting the brass lamp from the mantelpiece he polished the clear etched glass with his handkerchief. Then she watched with amusement as he carried it in the direction of their bedroom.

"Come, follow me. I think that there is nothing nicer than snuggling up in bed listening to a storm raging outside."

"Really! That sounds delightful, go ahead and I will be down in a minute."

She replied as she placed a screen in front of the fireplace. Apart from the glow from the hearth, she was now surrounded by darkness and she just happened to raise her eyes to the window. And there in the gap where the curtains met, she saw the shape of a face watching her. Rushing to open them fully she stumbled over a rug and by the time she reached the window, there was nothing to be seen but raindrops sliding down the glass against a black background.

"Sean, come here quickly."

Her voice shaking with fear echoed through the cottage and he bounded into the room.

"What's happened?"

"I could swear that there was a figure just a moment ago watching me through the window."

"Close those curtains and don't follow me no matter what happens. I want you to stay inside."

He whispered as he reached into a wooden box behind the table and took out his gun.

"Sean, be careful it may be a trap to get you outside, there could be any number of men out there."

Her heart felt as if it might explode at any minute.

"I can take care of myself. I will squeeze out through the small window at the side, if anyone is lying in wait for me, I can observe them from behind."

He was now speaking so low that she struggled to catch every word.

When the darkness of the hall engulfed him, she began to pray silently.

Standing as if frozen to the spot she waited and listened …. But all she could hear was the ticking of the clock and the wind howling at the gable wall.

When a blazing log slipped in the grate and send sparks flying into the air, she clutched the back of a chair and sat down slowly.

For over an hour she waited, staring into the flames and chiding herself for leaving her gun in her own house. In future, she would not venture to Aunt Rita's without it.

Just as she was trying to work out what to do if he did not return, she heard his key in the door and he appeared soaked to the skin but unharmed.

"When I raced out onto the road, I saw the glow from a cigarette just a couple of hundred yards ahead and I followed it for a couple of minutes. He knew I was trailing him because he stopped once and waited in the middle of the road in the pouring rain."

"Were there others with him waiting to pounce?" Sarah bit her fingernail with anxiety.

"No. I believe that he was alone, but I hid in the ditch just in case he had an accomplice.

At the crossroads, I lost him and so I wandered around in the swirling rain for a long time until I came upon a tinker's camp."

Sean paused for a few seconds while he dried his hair with a towel.

Sarah spoke as if to herself, "I don't care once - you are safely home."

"I would bet a pound that he was just a scout from that camp, looking for easy pickings."

"So, there is no cause for alarm, sit by the fire and I will get you some dry clothes. You don't want to catch a fever."

She hurried from the room exhaling loudly.

Much later, after two cups of scalding tea, she said,

"I remember Rita telling me that a big family of tinkers usually camp near the old ruin of the abbey for a few months every year."

Looking into the flames he swirled around the last dregs of tea leaves and said, "Good luck to them they pose no threat to us. You know sometimes I rue the night I pumped bullets through the two constables in the raid on Reelick barracks."

Sarah started to protest.

"Look, it's done …"

He interrupted. "I should have let them live. Then I could go about my business with the other IRA lads and not be on the run like some wild animal."

"Remember my dear Sean that had you not killed them first that they were about to kill you."

His countenance darkened.

"That's the story I tell myself, but the truth is that had we been more careful in planning the raid in the first place - there is the possibility that the constabulary would not have discovered our plans until it was too late."

"There really is no point in regrets. Besides, you would be six feet under now!"

"Who said that they would have killed me? I live with the fact that I snuffed out the lives of two ordinary decent men …. two fellow countrymen who were only trying to provide for their families."

This outburst made Sarah's face turn red.

"Well, if they did not shoot you there were two other options, languish in prison for years or swing at the end of a rope on some trumped-up charge. And I think that you have already had your fill of jail after months in Frongach camp."

Sean gave a devilish grin.

"Don't forget that I made some new friends there including Mick Collins and Billy O Connor."

She looked at him tenderly.

"Look what's done is done, at least you are free to carry on with your clandestine activities thanks to a coterie of men and women who risk life and limb for you. Not to mention the love of a good woman…"

Sean guffawed.

"Sarah … I would refer to you as a woman of many talents, but a good woman does not fit -how about feisty or indomitable?"

She gave him a mock punch in the chest and he took her in his arms and kissed her.

One week after, Sarah dismissed her pupils when the church clock chimed three times and as they streamed outside, she heard a commotion at the gate.

Suddenly, Bridie the most senior of her charges rushed in red-faced.

"Miss there is a tinker woman outside and she wants to come into the school. I told her that she was not allowed but she threatened to box my ears."

Sarah suppressed a smile.

"No wonder! Who gave you the authority to stop people from coming in?"

"The girl's face reddened further.

"My mother says that you cannot trust any tinker woman as they just want to get inside so that they can steal

- she gives them bread at the door and then sends them on their way."

"Well Bridie, you can tell your mother that not all tinkers are thieves and that everyone deserves a chance. Now go and invite that poor woman to come in and do not be so quick to judge in future."

"Sorry miss." The girl hurried off with her shoulders slumped.

A few minutes later Sarah heard a soft knock on the door and then a raucous voice exclaimed.

"The blessings of God on you Miss!"

She looked up from correcting sums to see a big, fat woman with weather-beaten skin and unkempt black hair. There was a strong smell of smoke which suggested that she had just left a campfire.

"Do come in and tell me what I can do for you," Sarah said gently.

"Thanks, that young brat wanted to turn me away. Can I take a seat somewhere, my feet are killing me."

Sarah pulled out a spare chair from the corner which she usually gave to the Parish Priest on his visits.

"Sit down and then begin."

"My name is Biddy-Anne Ward – I have a son called Bee; he is nearly a man. He can read but he cannot write. I had fourteen children, the two eldest went to Birmingham last year, they are bare knuckle boxers and Bee wants to join them. They are going hungry for the want of work and are in and out of jail, so I am told that if Bee goes too, he will end up in the same place if he has no book learning. My brother lives over there."

"My dear woman it will take time to teach your son to write, several weeks or indeed months and I doubt if you will stay that length in this parish. Also, who taught him to read?"

Biddy-Anne looked around the classroom for a few moments and then a silent tear fell from her right eye.

"Folk like us never get a chance, our young ones are not welcome in school. That's what I liked about old Master Seamus, he allowed all my young'uns, to attend school whenever we were in these parts and he taught a couple of them to read but there was no time to teach them to write."

Sarah's eyes narrowed.

"He is retired, but I am in charge and if I am to help your boy, you must do as I say, do you understand?"

"Aye, I will do anything you want."

Sarah studied her closely as she enquired.

"How many children live with you now?"

The woman hesitated as she began to count out names on her fingers. "Five died as babies, two live across the water, we got our three eldest girls married as soon as they could sleep with a man so that leaves four living with us in the wagon."

"Tell me about them." Sarah persisted.

The tinker woman began to lose her patience.

"Why are you asking me all this?"

Sarah turned slightly and looked out the window for a few minutes while the last group of her pupils sauntered down the road. Then turning quickly, she spoke in a sharp voice.

"I have seen women and young girls down-trodden for too long and if I am going to help your son then I might as well help your daughters as well, the world is changing fast and they will need the same skills."

"Well, the truth is that they too will be married as soon as they reach fourteen… apart from Bee there is Bernie aged twelve, Sally who is ten and the baby who is called Maisie."

"Right! If this is to work, I want to see Bee at school from next Monday morning. I will do my best to help him and if need be, I will take him for extra work on a Wednesday evening. Your other children are welcome to come too."

"Miss, leave them until next year, Paddy will beat me if I say they have to come here." Her small, narrow eyes filled with fear.

Sarah pulled a face, "Ok. There is no need to worry about books, copies or pencils as I have plenty here in the school but there is one condition which I must insist on -."

Sarah tapped her fountain pen on the table.

"What is it?" The tinker enquired acidly.

"Just that you take care to ensure that Bee comes to school with his face and hands washed, it is something that I apply to all my pupils."

Opening a drawer, she took out a large bar of home-made soap and old but clean towels. "Here take these I keep a supply for my special pupils."

Grinning to reveal several missing teeth, the woman blessed herself.

"The Good Lord sent you to this place, may he bless you with a good man and healthy children."

Sarah gave a weak smile and continued.

"I will do my utmost to ensure that he is not bullied but you must play your part by keeping him as clean and tidy as you can. It just happens that there are some spare funds left over from a recent donation to the school and I will leave a sum of money in Kennedy's drapery shop in the village so that you can bring him there and fit him out with new clothes."

The tinker woman beamed.

"Why are you doing all this for us? Miss, you are too kind!"

"No need to thank me. I want him to learn while he is at school, but he needs to fit in as much as possible with the others. An unhappy pupil will never learn anything!"

Reaching into the pocket of her baggy coat Biddy-Anne withdrew a holy picture of the Nativity scene.

"Take it, it will keep you safe from all harm."

Humbled by the woman's simple gift Sarah remained silent for a few moments.

Then regaining her composure, she spoke.

"Thank you so much for this. Where have you set up camp"

"We arrived last night and set up near the new forest, there is plenty of space there for our horses."

A thought flashed through Sarah's mind.

"By any chance did you stop about five miles outside Trim last week?"

She gave a loud cackle.

"Yes. My cousin and his big family are there. He has eight sons, a wife, a mother-in-law and his own mother plus an old tramp who joined them. Too many mouths to feed if you ask me, no wonder they are always getting into trouble with the local country folk."

Sarah started to flick through some copy books.

"Mrs Ward, you should go now as I have work to do."

The tinker woman gathered her plaid shawl around her ample bosom as she stood up straight. Then giving Sarah a crafty look, she made her way slowly to the door as she exclaimed.

"Miss if you ever want your fortune told come to me. My brothers are married to gipsy women from Liverpool and I learned a lot from them."

Leaning back in her chair, Sarah who did not want to appear rude replied.

"Thank you, I shall bear it in mind."

Shaking her head, the tinker responded drily.

"There is something wrong when a handsome young woman like you cannot get a man of her own. Maybe I could help you find one."

Sarah guffawed.

"Go on home and mind that brood of yours, I don't need a man."

Suddenly, Biddy-Anne stopped and turned around as if hit by a bolt of lightning.

"I feel it in my bones that you have a man, but you are not free to be seen with him, maybe he belongs in God's eyes to another woman or maybe he is a bad man who is in trouble -."

"Get out of here before I change my mind about teaching your boy, I don't have to listen to you spouting nonsense."

Sarah said reproachfully, as she banged her fist on the table. The tinker woman stuck out her tongue and then blessed herself before departing.

Sarah's knees were trembling when she bolted the door from the inside.

There was something in the tinker's bloodshot eyes that rattled her, as if she knew all her secrets.

Chapter Seven

Bee was a fast learner and injected energy into the class-room.

At fourteen years of age, he was almost six feet tall with piercing blue eyes and blonde hair. Even the parish priest, who had been charmed by him, remarked privately that he looked more like the son of some sailor from distant shores than the offspring of a tinker man.

Chuckling to herself Sarah had replied.

"Be careful! Biddy-Anne will give you a fat lip for casting doubt on her son's paternity!"

To her relief, the other pupils were struck by his humour and good nature, so in the playground there was always a group huddled around him, eager to join in pitch and toss or have their fortune told with cards.

In less than a month, he had reached an acceptable level of reading and writing, but he wanted to go further. He took to astronomy like a duck to water and delighted in hearing stories from Greek mythology about various constellations.

Yet he had a steeliness of eye which sometimes made her wary and there was a wildness about him which belied his interest in the written word.

She was not surprised when he failed to show up after a weekend break. However, when a whole five days went by and he was still absent, she decided to pay a visit to his family. In the gathering dusk of a November evening, an old woman with a billycan emerged from a cluster of trees. When she saw Sarah, she extended a grubby handful of tarot cards which she took from beneath her frayed shawl.

"Pick one." she urged, but Sarah walked briskly on along the rocky road until it eventually petered out into a dirt track that continued through the woods.

Her nostrils now filled with the smell of woodsmoke and she heard a cacophony of sounds. Hesitating for a few minutes she discerned the barking of dogs, a baby crying and a banging noise like a blacksmith working with metal.

"What do you want? You have no business in these parts!"

A hoarse male voice from behind a tree made her jump.

"I mean no harm, I came to see a young boy called Bee and his mother Biddy-Anne Ward."

"And who might you be?" A stocky man with a snarling black dog at his heels emerged.

"I am Miss Murphy, he attended my school for the last few weeks, he was doing so well with his writing and reading, he was very smart, everyone liked him, but he left without a word."

"Go home! When your type starts meddling, it always leads to trouble."

"Trouble! Is Bee in trouble?" Sarah enquired.

A coarse voice shouted.

"Johnny, I know her, I will deal with her."

Sarah turned to find Biddy with two little girls in ill-fitting clothes behind her. "I would like to speak with you for a few minutes, alone." Sarah ventured.

"Follow me."

The tinker woman took off at a fast pace with the children running along beside her.

In less than five minutes they reached a clearing in the woods where the glow from a log fire illuminated a group of men and women sitting in a circle. At one side she saw the outline of three or four wagons, while the smell of fresh horse dung hung in the air. Leading Sarah to the stump of an old tree nearby, Biddy-Anne sat on it while she directed the older child to fetch a stool from the wagon.

The child returned and said in a sing-song voice.

"Sit on it, miss!"

Sarah gave her a bag of currant buns which she had concealed in her bag.

"Thanks miss, I am starving!" The child ran off to share them with all the other children.

"That one is always hungry, no matter what she gets, her belly is never full," Biddy-Anne remarked.

"I want to ask you about Bee and why he suddenly left school, he was doing so well. If possible, I would like to talk to him myself."

Sarah's eyes had grown accustomed to the dark and she now realised that a man was sitting within earshot.

From deep in Biddy-Anne's chest a prolonged wailing sound emerged which made Sarah think for a few heart-stopping minutes that he was dead.

She struggled to say the words, "Is- is he gone?"

A voice from the shadows answered.

"If you think that he is dead you are mistaken, he was lifted last week by a bloody shower of men in uniforms!"

"Who?" Sarah asked in disbelief.

Another voice this time an old woman's explained.

"He means that the bastards from the local barracks came here at cockcrow and forced him to go away in chains, like a dog."

"Were they constabulary men?" Sarah's mind was racing as she tried to make sense of it all.

"Aye. Call them what you like. They took my handsome grandson, and they will be sorry when I am finished with them, there is no curse like a tinker's curse."

Her voice was thick with emotion.

"Why take him away?" Sarah exclaimed.

Biddy-Anne cleared her airways and spat out phlegm before she finally spoke.

"Because they say he stole a side of bacon from Tommy Keenan up at the hill farm."

Sarah persisted.

"Did he take it? And was there a reason?"

Biddy-Anne spat the words out.

"He was slaving for him at week-ends since we camped here but the only payment he got was in the form of a few turnips. Well, Bee is too brainy to let anyone make a fool of him and one evening he helped himself to a full side of bacon, he reckoned that it was owed to him."

"So, Keenan put the constabulary onto him," Sarah said softly.

"Aye. They came in here the following morning just as Bee was about to leave for his schooling. They got him by the ears and beat him black and blue, but he refused to tell them where he had hidden the bacon."

"I really am so sorry to hear such awful news," Sarah was filled with sadness.

"They took him away to the barracks in Dunshaughlin. He is in a cell there but if we can't pay the fine, the magistrate will order him to be jailed in Dublin."

Biddy-Anne wiped a tear from her eyes with the corner of her frayed old apron. Then in a sneering tone, she remarked.

"We had a mighty feast here last night, lovely juicy bacon with turnips, we knew that Bee hid it in the local graveyard."

Suddenly she cackled with laughter followed by a whole ripple of laughs from the shadows.

Sarah interrupted the mirth.

"How much time do we have before he is moved?"

A man reeking of tobacco smoke appeared from nowhere and tapped her on the shoulder.

"He has two days left, please help him, I am Jacksie his father, I don't want him sent to one of the jails in the city as he will be ruined mixing with robbers and murderers twice his age, he is just a boy."

Sarah stood up.

"I will do my best to get him out. Now you must promise me that when he is freed that he will leave here as soon as possible."

"My poor lad! Does he really have to go?" Biddy-Anne asked.

"The head man in the local constabulary does not like to have his plans thwarted so he will blame him for every theft or crime that occurs in this area. Mark my words, they will hound him until they put him in jail for a long time," Sarah explained.

Jacksie spat out some tobacco which he was chewing onto the grass, just missing Sarah.

"I heard he hates tinker because he says it was Gipsies who brought the Black Death from France to England."

"One way or another he hates tinkers," Sarah conceded.

Biddy-Anne interrupted.

"To hell with that jumped up old nobody! My brother's family camp every winter near Dublin city. Bee can go there and with a bit of luck he will work his way across to Liverpool on one of the cattle boats."

Jacksie added in a hoarse voice.

"Aye, the drovers are always looking for hands to help them drive the beasts from the cattle market across the city to the boat."

Sarah coughed loudly as her lungs struggled with all the smoke from the fire.

"I am leaving now but Jacksie you must meet me at the schoolhouse tomorrow when the children go home, as I hope to have news for you."

"I will be there Miss."

Then turning to a tall figure at the fire he spoke.

"Johnny, walk with Miss Murphy and don't take your eyes off her until she reaches home safely."

"You can count on me Uncle." The youth said proudly.

In less than twenty -four hours Sarah and Fr. Daly had gathered enough money from friends and acquaintances to pay Bee's fine.

He was released the following morning at dawn.

Following a farewell visit to his family, he did a last stop at the school to thank Sarah for her help. The pupils had made a hurried scrapbook for him in which they all wrote their messages of goodwill. By the time he left, there was not a dry eye among his old classmates. Even Sarah shed a few tears as she stood at the door and watched him walk through the school gates for the last time.

Out on the road, he stopped and shouted back.

"My ma said you are always welcome to call on her if you need help, she is a wise woman."

Then he whistled loudly as he squared his shoulders like a man and clambered across a stone wall. In less than half an hour he would reach the old Corpse road, an ancient route through Killeen to Dublin.

That evening Sarah was cycling to the village when a motor car passed her by, shuddering and shaking with clouds of black smoke erupting from under the bonnet.

A few hundred yards further on, it came to an abrupt halt and she saw two figures jump from it, seconds later there was a loud explosion and it burst into flames. Peddling furiously, she reached the scene and dismounted quickly where she found the two occupants dazed and confused after their lucky escape.

It was a few minutes before she realised that the man slumped at the ditch with the horseshoe moustache and bald head was, in fact, William Taylor the resident magistrate. Since his arrival in Meath, she had caught only fleeting glimpses of him, including the day he flashed by the school astride his chestnut mare and accompanied by other mounted hunters dressed in their hunting pink.

"Are you all right?" She enquired as he peered at her as if he had just seen a ghost.

She repeated the question but still, there was no reply, as he rubbed the sweat from his brow.

His chauffeur who was groaning with pain answered.

"Hurry to the village and get help, it looks like someone tampered with the car with the intention of killing us. I will see to his Honour, he is just in shock."

She nodded. "I will go as fast as I can."

In less than five minutes she arrived at the barracks where she reported the incident to an officer while his colleague took notes.

"Bloody IRA! He exploded.

"Did you see anyone else in the vicinity at the time of the explosion?"

"No, there was not another soul in sight. The car came from the direction of Tara. It passed me by slowly emitting clouds of noxious fumes and then further down the road it shuddered to a halt. Just before it exploded, I saw the two occupants escaping. That is all I can tell you."

A weak smile appeared at the corner of his mouth. "It was most fortunate Miss Murphy that you were cycling along and witnessed the whole thing. I will send a few men out there at once, you say that no one is hurt."

"I don't think so but Mr Taylor seems to be in shock."

She was anxious to be seen to be as helpful as possible as she did not want the finger of suspicion pointing at her.

"Right. You may go and thank you."

Then he took out a whistle from his pocket and blew it sharply.

"If I can be of further help you know where to contact me." She said in a matter of fact tone as he winked in her direction.

Minutes later, three men in bottle green uniforms rushed by her and took off in a noisy vehicle as she was making her way to the gate where she had propped her bicycle.

By the following morning, several RIC men from the nearby barracks were drafted in to make house to house searches in the hopes of finding the perpetrators of this heinous crime. Much to Sarah's relief the senior officer directed that her house be exempt given that she had already been through enough trauma by witnessing the explosion.

His Honour was examined by a doctor and found to have no injuries apart from a stiff neck and a bruised shoulder.

As the days turned into weeks rumours abounded about the identity of the culprits. Some whispered that they were disgruntled relatives of a prisoner, who had been sent by the magistrate to rot in a Dublin jail, while others pointed the finger at Sinn Fein.

Only Sarah who spent the following weekend with Sean was privy to the truth. He explained that a splinter group from the IRA branch near Mullingar had taken it upon themselves to kill the magistrate so that the RIC would clamp down on local branch members in Meath.

"The leader Morris Brennan has caused a lot of trouble in recent months for us and he decided that this would be the best way of making sure that we were all rounded up by the constabulary and incarcerated."

Sarah's face darkened as she tried to make sense of it.

"What will happen to him now?"

Sean gave a knowing wave of his right hand.

"It has been sorted."

"Oh, My God!"

She gasped as she ran her finger over the embossed label of the whiskey bottle in front of her.

Then she rounded on him.

"Why can't you just say that your lot killed him?"

Sean looked coldly out the window.

"He was taken to Ballivor bog and two of our men shot him. His family have been informed and he will have a Christian burial."

Sarah exploded.

"So according to your rule book, murder is fine once the victim gets to be buried in a Catholic graveyard!"

Sean remained silent but his jaws were rigid.

Sarah continued.

"Why not just warn him or send him on his way to America?"

"Come now," he said amiably. "You must see the predicament we were in, that turncoat was trouble. Sooner or later he would go to Dublin Castle and tell them everything he knew about our manoeuvres in Leinster."

Her voice was low.

"Did you give the order to shoot him?

Shifting in his chair he replied.

"He put the heat on this parish and on us, it was a stroke of luck that you happened to witness the explosion. The RIC has dismissed you from their enquiries because you reported the incident to them. It could have been much uglier."

"Did you or did you not give the order?"

"Yes," he conceded, with a slow shake of the head. "At least his death was instant, the others in the unit wanted to torture him first and then drown him like a dog."

Sarah felt sick.

"I am glad that I left Cuman na mban when I moved out here."

Sean raised his voice.

"Come now, Sarah. You knew when we got married that this is no pretend game of *Cowboys and Indians*. This is what real guerrilla war is like, it is dangerous and lives on both sides of the divide are lost."

"And that makes it all right to play God?" She said curtly. "Maurice Brennan leaves seven children and a wife. I knew him, he lived just a few streets away from Granny's house, his older brother used to go around with "the rag and bone man.""

Sean's eyes had a steely look in them.

"He changed … he was a loose cannon, there was no other way."

Sarah studied her husband.

"There is a coldness to you Sean Byrne and it frightens me!"

He jumped up and paced the floor for a few minutes.

Then with his back poker straight, he seemed taller than his six feet as he declared.

"I have never claimed to be a saint. And do you not realise that a fate worse than death would have been visited upon us if Taylor had died, the castle would have sent down their most brutal men."

Sarah considered this for a moment.

"I admit I got a shock when I realised it was Taylor who was lying at the side of the road. And I can't help thinking that it would be a small loss if he had been killed but - but such summary justice dispensed by you makes me wonder. Is it worth it?"

With a shake of his curly head, Sean opened the window and allowed the cool air to rush inside. A flock of crows were cawing as they gathered in the tall trees for the night.

"A typical woman! You cannot make up your mind one way or another."

"How dare you be so dismissive of women! Do I detect traces of misogyny?"

Sarah's voice was full of contempt.

"Just listen to yourself! You learned all that is to be known about guns from Cuman Na mbann. Did you think that it was all for amusement?"

"There is a big difference between learning to defend oneself and having random men from your own side shot."

Sean's right eye twitched as he replied

"Random man my foot! Brennan was trouble! He had a split personality. Schizophrenic I believe is the new name for his disorder, but I am no doctor."

"So, he was mentally ill! That makes his murder even worse."

Sarah fidgeted with a small, opal pendant at her neck.

"Well, if we did not murder him as you insist on calling it, he would have us murdered either by his followers or by the British bucks in Dublin Castle. My last word on this is that you are either for us or against us!"

She looked blankly past him at the long shadows of the trees.

He swept his hands dramatically through the air.

"What's the point in debating such matters at this stage?"

She remained silent, while he strode purposefully across the floor.

"I am going for a long walk."

Then, he went outside into the night.

She picked up his cigarette packet from the table and flung it in the direction of the grate, but it landed in a pile of logs at the side and the cigarettes scattered in every direction.

"Typical."

She exclaimed as a silent tear slid down her face, sometimes she wished that she were a million miles away from Ireland and all its troubles.

She could not get the image of Maurice Brennan's wife and children out of her head. She knew that they would ultimately end up in the workhouse, once the sum of conscience money which Sean and his cronies gave her ran out. She loathed how ultimately an innocent woman and children had to pay the price for the hubris of men.

The same question rattled around in her brain all evening.

How can men, who were once comrades-in-arms become bitter enemies with dire results?

The next morning at sunrise, She woke to see Sean shaving at the washstand with the light of an oil lamp.

She watched as he towel-dried his face vigorously.

"I hope to make it here by Christmas Eve! The sooth-sayers are predicting a white Christmas."

He kissed Sarah's sleepy cheek.

She sat up and pulled him closer as he kissed her lightly on the lips. Then looking into his eyes, she said.

"I love you, Sean. Take care!"

"I love you too Mrs Byrne!" He replied before giving her a final kiss, this time a long lingering one.

When he had gone, the eerie light of dawn crept into the room between the split in the curtains and she pondered over the previous night.

Shortly after their argument, Rita had returned home.

And when Sean reappeared after his stroll along the river, they all sat down together for a big meal, followed by fiddle playing from Sean and some tunes on the banjo from Rita.

Finally, when they retired to bed, Sean gave her a peck on the cheek and then turned his back on her. Sarah who never liked to let the sun go down without making up after a quarrel had pleaded with him.

"Sean, please turn around, I hate it when we fall out. I just want us to cuddle, nothing more! It will be days or weeks before we meet again."

His reply was acerbic.

"Leave me alone Sarah. I am very tired, and I want to sleep."

She had tossed and turned for most of the night while Sean slept soundly beside her. And as she listened to his regular breathing, she was reminded again of how she had chosen to build up a rosy picture of Sean as the handsome hero who was going to help bring about a free Ireland.

But a sly voice in her head had mocked her.

This is the real man you married.

Remember he was *described by some in Sinn Fein as having an iron hand in a kid glove.*

Suddenly, her mind returned to the present moment and the empty space in the bed beside her. She shivered in her light nightdress and swamped by feelings of loneliness, she decided to get up early and distract herself by making some scones for breakfast.

Although she struggled for some minutes to start a fire in the range, she knew it was better than listening to the awful doubt which kept surfacing in her brain.

Where will it all end?

Chapter Eight

In the build-up to Christmas Sarah did not have a spare moment. She organised whist drives and jumble sales to cover the cost of food boxes for the poor of the parish.

Much to the delight of her pupils, the Christmas holidays came earlier that year. She needed free days to oversee her helpers with the packing and delivery of boxes to the most vulnerable families. Her biggest problem was that the list of those in need seemed to mushroom by the day. In the end, she was guided by Fr. Daly who knew his flock like the back of his hand and could weed out chancers as he called them, a mile away.

Just as the soothsayers had predicted, by the twentieth of December the first flurries of snow arrived. At night severe frosts meant that everything from the large lake near Rosses to the local pond in the centre of the village froze. Given the extra difficulties in distributing the food to those who lived in remote areas, Sarah engaged the services of Tommie Black, a local man, who managed to deliver over fifty boxes by horse and cart.

She awoke early on Christmas Eve to a world covered in white.

At midday Tommie Black arrived, to take her to Rita's cottage. On the way, they made a detour to deliver a large box of food to the Ward camp in the woods. At first, it seemed like the camp had been deserted. A stillness encircled everything, and snow fell from branches high up in the trees to the ground below where a campfire usually blazed. Then just as she was about to leave the sound of voices from deeper in the woods reached her ears.

"Miss, may God reward you for coming all this way."

Sarah turned to see Biddy-Anne and a group of bedraggled children emerging from the darkness of the trees.

"Tommie will help you carry this box of food to someplace dry away from the snow," Sarah said.

The tinker woman rubbed her weather-beaten hands together with glee.

"Don't fret we can manage, we have plenty of places to store it."

Sarah could scarcely bear to look at the conditions in which they were forced to live but she managed a smile.

Biddy-Anne's chest heaved as she coughed up vile green phlegm and spat it out. "When the first snow arrived some days ago, we moved further into the woods where the wind can't hurl as much snow at us."

Sarah smiled.

"There is enough food there to keep you all going until the worst of the weather passes."

The older woman moved closer to Sarah and planted a quick kiss on her cheek.

"You have a beautiful face, full of goodness and kindness."

"My pupils don't always think so!" Sarah retorted, embarrassed by the woman's show of affection.

"Tell me do you have any news of Bee?"

The tinker's face lit up.

"Aye, news reached us that he is staying as planned with cousins at their camp near Dublin, he earns a few bob, by helping the cattlemen drive beasts from the market in Prussia Street to the cattle boats at the port."

"I am delighted to hear it. Now we must go before the weather worsens but take good care of yourselves."

Later at Rita's home, an inviting coal fire blazed in the hearth while they made the final preparations for a big feast on Christmas day. Although Sarah's hands were busy making the stuffing for the goose her mind was full of the image of the poor tinker family battling to get by in the snow. And she chided herself for not doing more for them.

Rita who saw her pensive expression tried to make her laugh.

"We will be fatter than that goose if we eat all this food."

"We might need every morsel of food if the snow drifts as we could be snowed in here for days," Sarah said abstractedly, while she peered through the window at the snow swirling around outside.

Rita nodded.

"I agree with you."

She had done all the preparations for Christmas. In the larder, there were two big puddings and a festive cake covered in almond and white icing like she had seen in the big houses. There were garlands of holly and ivy with cones from the forest hanging from the mantelpiece and above the dresser. While a bowl of expensive oranges from Valencia, which she had been given by the cook at nearby Remington Hall, formed the centrepiece on the table. And from each window, a red candle glowed to light the way not only for the Christ child but for Sean. She knew that Sarah was carrying around the last two letters from him in her handbag and she guessed that there had been some sort of a tiff between them at their last meeting because Sarah had made cryptic remarks about it.

Clearing her throat loudly, she said.

"Sarah, I am sorry, but I think that you should resign yourself to the fact that Sean won't be with us for the big day! The weather is closing in around us as I speak, there is no chance he could make his way undercover here in huge snowdrifts."

Sarah looked at her without saying a word.

"If he was not on the run there would be some chance of travelling by road but to go across fields would be perilous," Rita added.

Sarah said wistfully, "The sheer magic of Christmas when I was a child meant that one small toy like a rag doll provided me with days of fun and gave plenty of scope to my imagination. Sometimes I wish that my life could be a simple uncomplicated one. You know the IRA is getting more ruthless, they killed one of their own men killed recently and left his family to face the workhouse."

"There is no point in having regrets at this stage, in time you and Sean will settle down to a comfortable married life."

Rita wiped her hands on her apron and a cloud of flour rose into the air.

Sarah admitted, "I know it is not safe for anyone to be outdoors in this weather but especially Sean."

"Yes, better that he comes home late but safe," Rita remarked as she polished some much-treasured silver which only appeared for special occasions.

Sarah's voice dropped as she tried to hide her disappointment.

"I have to trust that he will be fine, he will hunker down in some safe house where they will play cards and drink bottles of whiskey. Once the snow starts to thaw, he will start for home and he will make it here before the New Year."

"Of course," Rita replied but deep down she doubted it. Going by what she had read in Old Moore's almanac, there were predictions that the snow would last for days.

On New Year's Eve, the mercury finally rose 2 degrees above freezing and the ice and snow slowly started to thaw. Sarah trudged a mile through the snow to Lackin's shop in the local village of Mounthill, where she bought as many groceries as she could carry. On the way home, she stopped at the church to light a few candles for Sean's safe return. Then she called at the baker's shop where the young apprentice told her of the awful tragedy which had occurred in Mounthill on Christmas Eve.

"Frankie Gleeson and his older cousin Eamonn Geraghty from Somerset went skating on Trasson lake outside the village."

Sarah felt a lump in her throat.

"I know Eamonn well, is he ok?"

The young man nodded.

"Eamonn survived but the lake was frozen over, there were several boys and girls on it having fun when the ice cracked under poor Frankie and he fell in and was drowned."

"Oh! That is terrible news. What age was Frankie?"

"He was just nine years old, a great young lad who was always dreaming about playing in Croke Park when he grew up."

Sarah shivered.

"How are his family coping with the loss of their child?"

The apprentice leaned forward across the counter and said in a conspiratorial voice. "Frankie's father is a blacksmith and Eamonn's father is a barber. Both have raging tempers and they blame Eamonn for taking the child onto the lake. But there were several others there too, even younger than Frankie-."

Suddenly Sarah felt as if she had been hit by some unseen assailant and it took her a few minutes before she ventured to ask what she sensed was coming next.

"Have they hurt him?"

The apprentice moved uneasily from one foot to another before replying.

"His father gave him a hiding and then boxed his ears so hard that they say he is now deaf in one ear."

Sarah could scarcely speak with shock she knew that Mel Geraghty was in a league of his own, when it came to punishment.

"Where -is Eamonn now?"

"Oh, I heard he is at home because he is not able to work in the forge due to all the bruising and swelling on his body. It was only yesterday that they managed to have a funeral for Frankie as the weather was so bad. He is buried up in the old graveyard at Creagh."

"Billy, stop that gossiping, get in here and do some work before I dock your wages."

The baker's voice boomed from a door behind the counter.

Sarah winked at him.

"Here's the money for the bread, you can keep the change. Now, go in before he clobbers you!"

She left the shop in a daze as a bell tinkled to indicate that she had departed.

One hour later when she finally returned to Rita's home she blurted out the sad news.

"What do you think I should do?" She asked.

Rita's voice was firm.

"Take my advice and do nothing. It is not your business. You do not want to draw the wrath of those two brothers upon yourself."

Sarah sat in front of the fire drying her feet.

"I just feel so sorry for Eamonn, he is neither a child nor a man. I wish I could help him."

Rita rubbed her hands nervously together.

"Stay clear of those bullies! You have enough on your plate."

At half-past twelve that night Sarah awoke to the sound of heavy rain on the eaves of the cottage. She listened for several minutes aware that something other than the weather had roused her. Throwing back the blankets she climbed from the big high bed and donned a dressing gown and slippers. Padding down the hall and into the kitchen she poked the embers in the hearth until there was a soft glow that cast shadows across the room. In that instant, she heard a tapping at the back door and went to investigate.

"Who is it?"

Her voice echoed through the darkness as Rita appeared in bare feet from her bedroom with half-opened eyes.

"Be careful!" Rita whispered as the faint tapping continued.

Unable to bear the tension any longer, Sarah ran to her bedroom where she grabbed her gun from under the bed. Then with the weapon in her hand, she directed Rita to open the door. There in the slush to her horror, she saw Sean slumped in a foetal position.

"Quick help me to lift him, he has passed out."

She deposited the gun on a chair. Then they managed to carry him indoors and laid him in front of the fire on a big sheepskin rug. Having removed all his wet clothes, she dried his body before putting pyjamas on him. While towel drying his hair, his eyes opened for a second and he muttered "Sarah - thank God."

She supported his head in her hands and he managed to take a few drops of lukewarm water but then he fell back into a deep sleep.

"He is exhausted, let him sleep, his body needs rest after hours of trekking through slush and rain." Rita declared.

Sarah tucked blankets around his body.

"What if it is more than exhaustion? What if he needs medical care? He is a wanted man, and we cannot risk bringing the local dispensary doctor here."

Rita dismissed the question with a wave of her hand.

"We will cross that bridge when we come to it. For now, he is safe and sleeping like a baby."

Sarah agreed.

"You are right, I will sleep here beside him for the rest of the night in case he needs anything. You go to bed and get some rest. Things won't seem so bad in the light of day."

Towards dawn, Sean sat bolt upright and shouted.

"Hands in the air."

Sarah who had not slept one wink calmed him down and reassured him that he was dreaming. He smiled at her and enquired.

"Where am I?"

She kissed him softly on the head.

"You are safe and well here with me. I made a bed beside the fire to warm you up. Now go back to sleep."

His face lit up for a moment as he spoke.

"My lovely Sarah, I - made it -home to you."

Then his eyes grew drowsy and he drifted back to sleep. Sarah, who checked his forehead and body for signs of fever, spent the remainder of the night applying wet cloths to his face and chest.

By the time Rita got up, she was worn out.

"I am terrified that he has caught some awful fever and will die."

Rita was determined to stay positive.

"He has no symptoms apart from the high temperature and he does not seem to be in any pain as he is sleeping peacefully. I think that we should try to get him to eat something like a soft-boiled egg with tea and soda bread."

Sarah's face brightened.

"I will give him another half hour while you are making breakfast and then waken him."

She found that it was easier than she had feared to rouse Sean, but he had to make three attempts before he could limp to the table for food.

"I just twisted my ankle. I fell on ice." He explained.

However, when he started to break the top of the egg with a spoon Sarah realised that he had little strength.

"When did you last eat?" She asked.

He frowned hard, "I can't remember, I don't even know what day it is. Have I been here a week or more?"

Sarah exchanged a glance with Rita.

"No. You came last night, just try to relax and eat something. You are exhausted."

After a few sips of tea and some mouthfuls of bread, he said.

"I want to sleep now."

They led him to the bedroom he normally shared with Sarah. When he had settled, they went back to the kitchen where they chatted in hushed tones about him over breakfast.

The next few days were rainy.

Sean spent most of the time in bed, but his appetite started to improve, and the sweating ceased. Towards evening, on the Friday, Sean declared that he was feeling much better and ready for a dinner.

To the relief of the women, he devoured a plate of roast chicken, cabbage and potatoes followed by custard and plum pudding. They all laughed when he licked the spoon to get the last of the creamy custard. He still had black circles around his eyes and a hoarse voice, but Sarah later confided in Rita that she was no longer worried about him.

Rita, ever the pragmatist, wondered if he was hiding something from them.

"I know the weather was atrocious and that he must have suffered a lot trying to reach here but he is reluctant to speak about any of it."

Sarah, who was abstractedly drying plates agreed.

"Yes, he is very quiet, not at all like his usual good-humoured self but he has just fought a fever of some sort without any medical help, that would leave him feeling low."

Rita fixed her eyes upon her.

"Only time will tell."

Over the next two days, Sean's health continued to improve and on Sunday night he announced that he would be leaving the following morning.

"Tonight, I am going to take out the fiddle and play a few tunes for my two lovely nurses, who brought me back from the brink of delirium," he said as his eyes twinkled.

Perched on a high stool near the fireside he beguiled them, first with jigs and reels then some pieces from Bach and finally, he gently plucked the strings as he softly sang a haunting old love song. Both women had tears in their eyes by the time he finished.

To applause and laughter, he laid his instrument down and they all raised their glasses to toast his health and the new year of 1920, still in its infancy.

Perhaps it was the whiskey combined with the deep emotions which the beautiful music had stirred. Or maybe it was the trials of recent days when she had nursed him back from the brink or simply the fact that they had not enjoyed the pleasures of each other's bodies for several weeks. Whatever the reason, there was an intense and heady yearning between them that night.

And even after hours of intimacy, their lust for each other had not been quite satiated.

At precisely eight am when the distant sound of the church bell from the village could be heard in the still morning, they made love all over again.

By midday, Sean had departed, dressed as an old beggar man, a disguise he sometimes used if he needed to change his route and venture by the outskirts of villages and towns until he reached Shalvey's safe house.

There, he would meet with members of the IRA who had many ingenious ways of transporting him to meetings in the midlands and beyond, without attracting unwanted attention.

Chapter Nine

Never had the reopening of the school after the Christmas holidays been so welcome, not even as a newly qualified teacher had she been so pleased to return to teaching. When she unlocked the heavy school door and saw the neatly stacked shelves of books and copies alongside orderly rows of desks, a sense of calmness enveloped her. Here she was in charge, here she could reward hard work, plan lessons for her pupils, and provide a safe, caring environment where she strived to treat each child equally, regardless of background or ability.

On the contrary, her personal life seemed more tumultuous than ever. Sean had indicated on his last morning that he would be seeing less of her than ever as the IRA was planning to step up its activities nationwide. She knew instinctively what this entailed, more cattle-runs, more so-called seditious meetings, more raids on barracks for arms, inevitably leading to more loss of lives on both sides. He had even given her the name of a safe house near the city centre, in the event that he disappeared and all letters from him ceased. The Mulroy family would be well placed to help her, given that all the siblings were active in the organisation. In the days that followed, Sarah threw herself wholeheartedly into her teaching and extra-curricular tuition. With eight pupils to be confirmed by the Bishop in late spring plus an end of year play to be written and approved by the Parish Priest, she was inordinately busy.

One night in early spring, Sarah took advantage of the bright, starlight sky. She hummed to herself as she went to her bedroom where a telescope on a stand pointed heavenwards. Whenever she felt troubled, she always turned to stargazing as it helped to calm her. Looking for new stars and grappling with how that light which she was witnessing had left its source at least a thousand years earlier, helped her to focus on what really mattered and reminded her to take each day as a gift.

As midnight approached, she paused and moved to the window, outside the garden was bathed in moonlight. She was just about to close the curtains when her right eye caught a flicker of light from underneath the hedge. She knew instinctively that someone was out there, someone who had just lit up a cigarette with a match and then blown it out. And if she strained her eyes hard, she could still see the glow from the top of the cigarette.

For a moment she stood as though transfixed, could this mean that he or she wanted to be seen. Drawing the curtains quickly, she got her gun. Then as she was walking the length of the hallway, she heard a voice calling from outside the front door.

"Miss Murphy, it's Eamonn Geraghty, please don't be frightened I just need to talk with you, I have no one else that I can trust."

For an instant, she considered sending him home but given the recent tragedy in his family and the subsequent beating which he had received she knew that his plea for help was genuine. Hiding the gun behind a coat on the hall stand, she drew back the heavy bolts and unlocked the door quickly.

"Step inside. Is there any chance that you have been followed?"

He shook his broad young shoulders.

"My old fella is playing poker down in Haverty's and everyone else is in bed."

She noticed that he seemed to have grown a few inches since their last meeting and she calculated that he must be well over 6ft. tall.

"I apologise but I am desperate to leave that mad-house," he explained, as she relocked the door.

Then she led him to a seat by the fire where a few dying embers still glowed.

Sitting directly opposite she lit the oil lamp and then studied his face.

"I am risking everything by talking with you, so I need total honesty."

Eamonn ran a hand across his forehead.

"I swear that I am not here to cause you any trouble, I just want to get away from my father before he kills me. No doubt you heard all about my cousin drowning and that I was blamed for his death."

"Indeed," she said gravely.

Lifting-up his thick Aran jumper and woollen vest he revealed his back. It was obvious even to her untrained eye that he had taken a severe beating with wounds still visible from his shoulders to his waist. Biting her lower lip to prevent herself from adding to the boy's anger she chose her words carefully.

"This is appalling treatment to be meted out by a father to a son. I am so sorry that you have suffered in this way, now tell me about your plan."

He cleared his throat nervously.

"I think you know that the old fella takes money from the constabulary to carry tales back to them about his neighbours. I hate him, if I don't get away I will kill him. He could have beaten me to death with that vicious temper and I still have a loud ringing in my ears after the boxing he gave them."

Sarah clenched her fists, angry that Callaghan thought so little of his own son.

"You are right I think you need to go before he does kill you as he is out of control. Is it money that is stopping you?"

Leaning forward, he spoke in a conspiratorial tone.

"No. I don't just want to run away and lose myself in England or beyond. I still love books and mathematics, but I want to make a difference. You said yourself that I am intelligent -."

"Be specific! What exactly do you want from me?" Sarah asked impatiently.

"I am the direct opposite to my old man who is a traitor. I love my country and I despise the British, the time is over for talking. First, the Volunteers and now the IRA are building up to a war, you know this Miss."

Sarah felt like an icy wind was gripping her body, but she feigned innocence.

"I know little or nothing about such activities, I am a schoolteacher."

"It is time to stand up and fight. Too many years have been wasted, the day of the Home Rulers is past." He gave her a knowing look.

Sarah noticed that his face was purplish-red in colour and his right foot rocked back and forth on the old floor as if he were about to explode.

"If you have something else to say spit it out."

She met his eye unflinchingly, but her heart was pounding because she sensed what was coming.

"I don't mean to be impertinent but I have been following you since the time you stopped me from attending your evening classes."

Sarah exploded.

"You cheeky brat! Some weeks back, I knew there was someone lurking outside."

"I am so sorry Miss but – but I look up to you. I know that you have a sweetheart who is on the run – and that he is in the IRA because I have followed him too. I want to join up with his men."

For a few minutes, it seemed to Sarah that her world had just been blown apart. A shiver ran up her spine and her head pounded while her throat seemed so tight that words would not come.

"Miss – Miss, you look as white as a sheet, I hope that you are not going to faint."

His voice was full of concern.

She stood up slowly and looked directly down at him.

"Is this some form of blackmail? How dare you spy on me!"

"No -No- No. I know that it was wrong to follow you and your man, but I sensed that you were in great fear of my father and I had to discover the reason. I guessed that you were covering something which he could report to the constabulary, but I swear I am genuine about my desire to join up."

Her blood ran cold, but she responded in a matter-of-fact voice as she could not allow him to see the effect his confession was having on her.

"Well, aren't you a smart young fellow!"

"Miss, I am begging for your help, you have to believe that I am genuine."

He dug his fingernails into his palms.

"How can I ever trust you? You are no better than your father, spying on me."

A great primaeval wail escaped from him as he got down on his knees and then pleaded with her.

"Oh my God, I am not like him at all, I am so ashamed of him and his two-faced ways."

In the faint light, with eerie shadows dancing on the walls she could not see his features clearly but studying his demeanour she knew instinctively that he was not just playing a part.

Adopting a schoolmarmish tone, she asked.

"How many others know about your spying activities on me?"

He stood up to his full height and tears cascaded down his face.

"In the name of God, I swear that I have not told another soul about you."

Sarah countered.

"Your so-called findings on my private life could curry favour for your father with the men at the top, or you could just go to the castle yourself and spill your guts!"

In a voice filled with shock, he made the sign of the cross.

"Upon my word I will never betray you, you have been so good to me."

For several minutes there was silence while Sarah tried to work out the import of his words.

Then he spoke.

"Someday, I hope that those English men in Dublin Castle will turn on him and that he will hang by the neck. I have nothing but respect for you Miss Murphy, I am desperate to get away, but I don't just want to run away to sea like my old schoolfriend Kevin Mc Donald did last year, I want -to do something with my life."

Eamonn wrung his hands in desperation.

Her brain was working feverishly, the way she saw it now, there was no real option except to take Eamonn at his word and refer him to some of Sean's men who could train him in IRA tactics. If she turned down his request, he could jump ship and reveal all to the constabulary but first, she intended to make him sweat. She was relieved that he did not seem to know Sean's actual name or the fact that they were married.

"It is preposterous that you would just turn up here and demand to be allowed to join the IRA. Firstly, I fear that you are full of idealism, after all, you just turned 15 recently and secondly, you have watched my comings and goings to the extent that you even followed me to my relative's house."

He snorted.

"I never got the chance to be a carefree child, removed from the harsh reality of the world. I had to grow up fast. There was always a war of some sort in our house, my old fella saw to that."

Sarah looked at him with the air of an inquisitor.

"What is your answer to the fact that you spied on me?"

Eamonn's face crumpled.

"I did not see it as spying, at first I was curious to see why you were so terrified of crossing my old man. And I watched you for seven different nights, eventually, I started to follow you over to your relative's house. Then on the second weekend, a man appeared who was obviously in hiding from the authorities, so I realised that I was onto something big. Do you recall the night your sweetheart followed me to the outskirts of the tinkers camp?"

Sarah lit a second lamp as the embers in the grate died. "Yes."

He nodded as a thin smile played around his eyes.

"I stood in the middle of the road for a few minutes in the hope that he would approach me as I view him as a hero but then I lost my courage and ran away."

"I see. What about the time I caught you red-handed in this house, were you really looking for books or were you spying?"

He protested vehemently.

"I was not spying at that stage on you, I can swear it on a bible if you like. I wanted to get my hands on your advanced books."

Sarah rubbed her forehead and then moved closer to him as she stared into his eyes.

"It puzzles me that you do not go along to one of the Sinn Fein meetings in Navan and tell the top lads about your wish to join in the fight for freedom."

He harrumphed.

"They would never believe that the son of an informer would really wish to join them, they would see it as a snare or trap and so I could not risk it," he said with the air of someone much older.

"Don't you mean entrapment?" She said harshly.

He nodded.

"Aye, that's the word, I want to get on in the world and not be stuck in ignorance forever."

Then she looked at him with a mixture of consternation and compassion.

"You have an answer for every question, and you have a maturity beyond your years. I only hope and pray that you are telling the truth because if this is some convoluted double-cross the IRA will kill you themselves. They can be ruthless and cold-blooded and let me tell you there is no place for idealistic young boys among them."

"I know! I am telling the full truth and I am at your mercy."

He said as he bowed his head and wept.

Sarah couldn't bear to see the poor fellow suffer any longer, while the wall clock loudly ticked away the minutes, she devised a plan.

"Before I go any further, you must promise me that you will not return here to my cottage again or indeed to the school, I cannot risk your father finding out -."

Her voice shook slightly.

He dried his eyes with a grey handkerchief and then blew his nose hard.

"I promise on my young cousin's grave that I will do as you ask."

"Well then, I want you to go home now and act as if nothing has changed. Tomorrow night when they are all in bed you will cycle to Kilmessan station, then you will follow the railway line on foot as far as Dunboyne."

"Yes, Miss. I will do everything you say."

"Anyone will direct you to the village of Collmore where the Parish Priest lives in a two-storey house on the fair green. Beg him to hear your confession, you should arrive at his house before noon if all goes well, then tell him everything."

"Confession! I am not a very religious person!"

Sarah shook her head with exasperation.

"I don't care if you believe in a divine power or not! You should know that the priest is bound by the seal of confession and cannot repeat what you confess to him."

He suppressed a heavy sigh and looked at her in surprise.

"So, do I tell him everything even about you Miss Murphy?"

"He knows about me, he is a sympathiser, and he has two brothers who are leaders with the movement. He will put you in touch with them. You look older than your years, no doubt you will be trained and sent on active duty to Munster or Connacht where no one can recognise you."

He swallowed.

"I am so grateful to you Miss. Thank you for everything."

She took out a few coins which she had stored in an old jar on the dresser.

"Take these, you will need them for food on your journey. Remember that if the plan fails you must not reveal your connection with me to anyone other than the good priest."

He put the money in his pocket as he answered.

"I would rather die than get you into trouble, I am not my father's son!"

She tapped him on the shoulder.

"Be careful Eamonn, you may be taller than many men twice your age, but you are so young and have so much to learn. Alas, the world is not black and white - now go!"

She turned and led the way through the passageway. When she opened the door, he hesitated for a moment and leaned towards her.

"Goodbye Miss, without your help I would have killed myself."

Sarah did not reply, but she squeezed his hand, as she was fighting to keep back the tears at the corner of her eyes. In seconds, he had disappeared into the long shadows of the trees. Shaking all over, she bolted the door carefully and then rechecked it. In the kitchen, she reached for a bottle of brandy because she needed to calm her nerves and blot out the question which swirled around in her head.

Have I just signed my own death warrant?

Chapter Ten

Two days later, Sarah stood before her class, bleary-eyed and nauseous.

She had not had a decent night's sleep since her midnight conversation with Eamonn. Sometimes, in the middle of the night, she awoke with a start and got up to check that there was no one prowling about inside the cottage. Then, returning to the warmth of her bed, her mind replayed word for word the conversation which she had had with him.

Now, she must exert herself for the sake of the children sitting expectantly at their desks with their eyes watching her every move.

"Infants and senior infants do some colouring while the rest of you can draw a picture from nature: like lambs or even birds busy building their nests."

Mary Kate Tuohy stood up and protested.

"Miss I am not good at drawing."

Sarah interrupted her.

"Sit down at once! Anyone who does not wish to draw a picture is free to write an essay about spring."

A wave of whispers spread through the room and she warned them to be quiet as she enlisted the help of two senior girls to pass around paper and pencils followed by crayons or colouring pencils. Once a hush had descended on her pupils, she sat at her desk marking copy books, but five minutes later, her mind wandered, and her head ached.

Abandoning her task, she took out a small writing pad from the press along with blue carbon paper for copying. Then she wrote a coded letter to Sean in which she apprised him of what had happened that fateful night with Eamonn. Unsure of Sean's whereabouts, she would send two letters. The original one to a safe house in Mullingar and the copy to a similar place of hiding near Athlone. She would post them as soon as school ended in the village Post Office.

At precisely eleven o 'clock she allowed the children out to play in some unexpected sunshine, while she poured over a recent copy of the *Freeman's Journal*.

The front page proclaimed that the RIC were losing their grip on the country due to the thousands of civilians who were now joining the IRA to engage in guerrilla warfare.

The editorial proclaimed; 'The British Secretary of State for War, Winston Churchill is scrambling a special Reserve Force who will assist the constabulary in restoring order to Ireland.'

Sean had warned her that harsh moves were afoot to put down the Irish troublemakers. She felt like someone had just walked on her grave as she recalled the hatred which she had observed in his eyes while he recounted this to her.

Suddenly, her attention was drawn to the sound of a commotion in the schoolyard. She hurried outside to find Mel Geraghty kicking young Philip Regan from fourth class while his older brother Tommy tried to intervene.

"What is going on here? Mr Geraghty, you must stop this behaviour at once or I shall have to call for help from the barracks."

He turned to face her and sneered.

"Call them if you like, they will believe me. Who would rely on the word of a child or a man-hating school teacher?"

She spoke with authority.

"Philip and Tommy go inside, and I will look after you in a few minutes. Now, sir, you have not answered my question yet!"

His mouth formed an ugly sneer.

"To hell with those brats they nearly knocked me over. Let us get down to business, you know why I am here."

"Come now, they were only playing tag it was not intentional. And to put you straight I have no idea why you are here disrupting my pupils."

He stepped closer to her and fixed his eyes upon hers with a look that reminded her of a dog about to kill a rabbit.

"Where is Eamonn? I know that you are involved in his disappearing act."

Feigning innocence, she replied.

"Disappearing act? Do you think I am Harry Houdini? Besides, I had no idea that Eamonn is dabbling in magician's tricks!"

He raised his fist and shouted.

"Don't play clever with me! You know well that he ran away during the night, some of his belongings went with him. He did not show up for work this morning either."

Sarah shook her head.

"I had no idea. Maybe he just took a day off from his routine at the forge, the work there is hard for a young lad. He will be back before dark."

He glowered at her suspiciously.

"I will ask you one last time. Where is he hiding? Is he in your cottage?"

"In my cottage! Are you mad? Come with me after school and check it if you wish. I know nothing about your son."

Apoplectic with rage he roared as the children scattered in every direction.

"You will be sorry for meddling in my affairs and for filling my boy's head with notions. Be warned, if he does not show up in the next few days there will be trouble."

Her throat felt constricted and her stomach was heaving but she managed to say.

"Good day to you, I hope you find him, but I have children to teach."

In the days that followed, news of Eamonn's disappearance spread quickly throughout the whole parish and beyond. The streets and shops were awash with rumours about his fate, not since the failed Easter Rising and the battle of Ashbourne had any occurrence grabbed the attention of every man, woman, and child

Some whispered that he had been murdered by his own father, more believed that members of the local constabulary had him shot and then dumped in a lake because Mel Geraghty had in some way duped them. While others swore that eyewitness accounts put him at the port of Drogheda, on the first stage of his journey to Liverpool and thence to America.

Wherever Sarah went, from the grocery shop to the cobblers, gossip abounded about Mel Geraghty's temper and his duplicitous nature. Through it all, she tried to remain calm but engaged as if the boy's disappearance was as much of a shock to her as to everyone else.

Even in the playground, the older children huddled in groups, telling tales of what had become of Eamonn.

At Sunday mass prayers were offered for his safe return and it was decided by a group of concerned parents, that a search party would comb the fields, woods, bogs, riverbanks, and local lakes. Sarah, who had to be seen to cooperate, suspended school for two whole days. And she joined a group to explore every inch of the surrounding countryside while his poor mother languished in bed, according to the gossip mongers like one possessed, shouting.

"My poor lad killed himself, may the Lord have mercy on his soul."

By the following Sunday, after some pleading from Mel Geraghty, three burly men from the constabulary made door to door enquiries but all they met with were blank stares.

On that same day, Sarah cycled to Rita's for a short visit to fill her in on recent happenings. She had decided that for the foreseeable future she would no longer spend alternative weekends there because they could not be sure until they heard from Sean that Eamonn had managed to get safely to the IRA house near Dunboyne. She could not bear to even think that he had been kidnapped and forced to reveal all about Rita's "safe house" and Sean's regular rendezvous with Sarah there.

Rita, who was concerned about Sarah's safety but was without any thought for her own, volunteered to make her way to Sarah's house every fortnight instead.

Sarah hugged her.

"My dear Rita, it is so kind of you to offer but don't you see that it might be wiser for us to take a break altogether. If Eamonn spills the beans, then not only will my place be watched but so will yours. However, if I have no contact with you for some weeks, at least until I am sure that Eamonn has joined up safely with the men, then no harm can come to you."

"Why would they waste their time with an old woman like me?" Rita asked.

"That's the point, they won't unless they see that I am still staying over there with you regularly. Otherwise, they will just focus on my cottage as they will reckon that Sean will show up there sooner or later."

Rita protested.

"I hope that Sean does not call on you, it is too danger-ous. Besides, what about you, there on your own?"

Sarah turned up her nose.

"Don't worry! I wrote him a coded letter as soon as it all unfolded, he won't show up here or at my home either. And I too will be safe because they won't touch me until they have found Sean, I guess I could be viewed as a type of bait."

Rita was quiet, while she struggled to make sense of it all.

Then Sarah, feeling guilty about loading her troubles on her, tried to allay Rita's fears.

"It's all just hypothetical. You know me, I am a stick-ler for detail. I am confident that Eamonn made it safe-ly to his destination and is now being trained with the IRA, in which case I am making a mountain out of a molehill."

Rita folded her arms against her body.

"I hope that you are right. Of course, I will go along with what you say about keeping our distance, but it can-not go on indefinitely."

Sarah kissed her on her forehead.

"Thanks for being so understanding. I asked Sean to send a brief note to me at my own cottage under a pseud-onym, just to confirm that he is safe and up to date with events but so far I have heard nothing."

Rita gave her a maternal look of tenderness.

"Don't fret, a note will arrive soon from him, he knows how to take care of himself."

They were seated at the table which was laden with food and Sarah helped herself to a slice of sponge cake while Rita made more tea.

"Oh, this cake is so light and so delicious!" Sarah said.

"But what about the cold meat and the eggs, are you not going to have some?"

Rita's face was clouded with disappointment.

Sarah, who did not want to offend her, lied.

"I am sorry Rita, but I made a glutton of myself this morning, bacon, eggs, sausages, and fried bread. Please forgive me, I can see that you went to a lot of trouble."

Rita pursed her lips together in a smile.

"You are forgiven! I don't mind once you are eating good food as you will need plenty of energy to deal with all that's happening in your life at present."

She hated lying to Rita, but she did not wish to burden her with more worries.

For five mornings in a row, she had experienced bouts of retching and had stopped eating breakfast. This seemed to make no difference as her stomach muscles failed to recognise that her stomach was already empty and that there was nothing left to throw up. She had had food poisoning before and no matter how much she wracked her brain could not work out which food in her larder had been contaminated. She had resolved that if the spasms in her stomach did not stop in the coming day or two that she would have to go to the dispensary doctor.

"A penny for your thoughts?" Rita joked as she interrupted Sarah's musing.

"They are not worth it! I was just daydreaming. Now, please give me the recipe for this delicious cake, I cannot make a proper sponge, they are always as flat as a pancake."

By the time she reached home that evening, she was exhausted. Even though the journey there by bicycle was mainly downhill and she had cycled it hundreds of times, she could hardly keep her eyes open due to tiredness.

At 8 pm she went to bed and slept soundly until the voices of children laughing, on their way to serve at early mass the next morning woke her. She felt much better and decided to make a good breakfast of porridge, boiled eggs, and brown bread. She had always loved food and its preparation and happily spent the next half hour cooking. However, as soon as she had eaten it, she was seized by bouts of retching and had to run out into the garden where it seemed that even the lining of her stomach would be expelled. Exhausted, she went back inside and sat in an old armchair for the remainder of the morning while she tried to take in the latest news from *The Freeman's Journal*.

It was reported that thousands of the special temporary constables recruited to assist the Royal Irish Constabulary were on their way to the country. Given the increasing attacks on rural stations and the mounting pressure on RIC men and their families, many were resigning having witnessed their colleagues being injured or killed.

The new arrivals would help swell numbers in fewer, heavily fortified stations and put an end to the mayhem of cattle drives and ammunition raids on local more isolated stations. Sarah shivered as she read that many of the new recruits were British Army veterans of the Great War. The report went on to say that their improvised uniforms would be composed of mixed khaki British Army and rifle green RIC uniform parts.

With a sinking heart, she knew that it could only mean even stronger resistance from the IRA and more danger for Sean.

Turning to the next page her eyes inspected the column of advertisements.

Castor oil for hair loss.

Glauber salts for constipation.

Dunn's Pure fruit Saline for relief of morning sickness.

She leaned forward in her chair while her whole body stiffened.

Then the print seemed to jump off the page as she read and reread the last two words. Suddenly, it all made sense, the fatigue, the retching, and the malaise.

They were all the tell-tale signs of early pregnancy. And she recalled the long night of lovemaking with Sean when she had thrown caution to the wind, ignoring all the rules which she had learned from Maddie's books on birth control.

She shoved her chair away from the fire and cursed as she got to her feet. Then padding to the bedroom, she removed her clothes and examined her belly from every angle in the mirror. However, she could not see any difference in the shape of her body apart from her breasts which seemed bigger than usual. For a few minutes she stood transfixed while tears coursed down her face, she could not have conceived at a worse time.

The IRA were stepping up their military actions which meant that Sean was less available than ever to her and she would have to leave her position as schoolmistress at the end of June, once a bump began to show. The fact that she had posed as a single woman had now come back to haunt her because the priest and his parishioners would view her as a scarlet woman who was a bad example to children and young people.

Dressing slowly, she wished that she could turn the clock back to that night when she had been so cavalier about having unprotected sex. Now, it was too late, and she felt overcome with tension and a sense of panic.

At that moment she heard the brass knocker echoing through the cottage. Taking a comb, she hurriedly tidied her hair and replaced the hairpins which had fallen from her bun. Then smoothing her clothes over her stomach, she walked slowly to the door and opened it. "Miss Murphy, are you all right? You look like you have just heard a banshee!"

Mrs Ward the tinker woman stood there with an empty basket in her hand.

Sarah answered with a grim countenance as she beckoned to her to step inside.

"I am fine."

The weather-beaten face relaxed into a wry smile, revealing yellowed and broken teeth.

"We are leaving tomorrow and heading over to my brothers camp near Ashbourne, I just wanted to say thanks for everything."

Giving her a friendly pat on the arm, Sarah enquired.

"Have you heard from Bee? Did he make it to England?"

The woman grinned from ear to ear.

"Only last week, I met Tommy Connors who is just home from England. He saw Bee in Liverpool working at the docks. And he is hoping to go to America, he can cover the price of his passage across the Atlantic by working on one of the big ships."

"That is good news. He is a fine young man," Sarah replied.

A smell of woodsmoke emanated from her worn shawl as her face flushed with pride.

"Any other year we would be travelling the roads of Westmeath and Longford once the first lambs arrived, but we did not want to leave until we heard that he was safe."

"Would you like some food?"

Sarah enquired, as she noticed the tinker woman's eyes wandering over her rack of spices.

"Aye, I would, you know the winter was a bad one and we could not have got by without all those food parcels you sent over every Wednesday night."

"Thanks to everyone in the parish who contributes to the food boxes, it's not just me, you know," Sarah explained.

"Well, I know that you are the head of it along with the man of God, the priest."

Five minutes later, Sarah had filled the tinker's basket with a block of cheese, eggs, bread, and a slab of fruit cake.

"The blessings of God on you and that little one in your belly," she exclaimed.

Sarah stared at her with an expression of disbelief.

Before she could reply, Biddy-Anne continued.

"Don't look so shocked Miss, when your belly has carried as many babies as mine, you learn how to know when there is another one on the way. There is a look in your eyes and the pallor of your dial that gives it away."

Sarah held onto the back of the chair with her two hands while she recovered from the shock.

For a few minutes, there was silence as the tinker arranged the food in her basket.

Then Sarah spoke.

"I am disappointed that you are so disrespectful. How dare you peddle lies about me. I have had a sick stomach for the last few days, but it is due to some form of food poisoning as I ate meat which was gone off. Now, please be on your way."

"But I mean you no harm Miss, I just know the signs so well myself that I was trying to be helpful as I can see you don't know yet that you are expecting."

Sarah swept down the hallway and held the door open for her.

"It's all mumbo jumbo, real gipsy talk! Like the fortune tellers at the fairs who tell every woman they see that they will soon hear wedding bells and the patter of little feet."

The tinker woman followed her but hesitated before going outside.

"You think now that I am just a fool, but time will tell - I know what it's like to be chased out of town so if you ever need a place to hide you can come to us."

Sarah's mouth fell open at the audacity of the tinker, who was gazing at her.

Then, after a few seconds, she managed to say stiffly.

"I wish you and your family Godspeed."

Undaunted, Biddy-Anne touched Sarah's shoulder affectionately.

"Goodbye and good luck!"

In a flash she was gone, leaving Sarah standing forlornly at the door for some minutes.

She watched as two pigeons squabbled over some crusts which she had discarded earlier. Then in the blink of an eye, a large-hooded crow swooped down and devoured the lot while the two opponents scattered leaving a cloud of feathers. Chuckling at their folly and the beauty of nature all around, she suddenly felt overwhelmed by the idea that she was carrying a new life. Touching her belly tentatively, she went inside to make a nice rich cup of cocoa with hot milk.

Chapter Eleven

The following morning, Sarah rose early and swallowed a concoction of tonic water, peppermint, and ginger. It was an old recipe of her grandmother's which she hoped might help with morning sickness. Afterwards, she managed to keep down a cup of tea and bread which she toasted at the open fire with a toasting fork. It was the first morning in days that she felt well and able to cope with the different needs of her pupils. Later, when it was time to send them home, she stood at the door and observed the children as they trooped down the path to the main gate, amidst a deafening assortment of laughter, shouts, and whistles. Once outside, the older girls chatted animatedly to each other in twos and threes as their counterparts, the older boys engaged in horseplay. It was different with the younger pupils, some linked arms with their pals and huddled together in small groups while others straggled after their older siblings. Touching her abdomen lightly she wondered about the baby growing inside her and whether it was a boy or a girl. She had decided to keep her pregnancy a secret even from Rita at least until she managed to tell Sean.

The evenings were the worst, sometimes after tea, doubts niggled her concerning his safety, so she immersed herself in watercolours. Filling a large canvass with tiny flowers and several species of birds which she had seen in the bog. And she often wondered about her love of art and if she had inherited it from her absent father but then she would quickly dismiss such thoughts, reminding herself that he had not even bothered to make contact even after her mother's tragic death.

On Saturday she boarded the early train from Kilmessan Station to Dublin, followed by a tram to Clerys store on Sackville street. In their extensive lingerie department, she chose two heavily boned corsets. She knew how the local women in the village would gossip if her stomach started to swell and she did not want a confrontation with them or the priest.

Instead, she planned to conceal her pregnancy until the term ended and she was miles away from Meath. She also bought three large brassieres because her breast size had increased in recent weeks. Next, she walked to Halligan's chemist on the quays. Coughing and choking, she covered her mouth with a handkerchief to avoid the thick black fumes coming from the motor cars which were competing for space on the streets alongside horses, bicycles, and trams. Outside the chemist, Sarah aware of her ringless finger paused to put on gloves while a nursing mother huddled against the wall surrounded by five little urchins.

Sarah gave the oldest girl a sixpenny bit and ordered her to buy ha'penny buns for them.

"Ta miss, I will go to the corner shop, we are starving with the hunger."

The girl shouted before running down the street. Inside the chemist, Sarah's eyes were attracted to the rows of glass bottles lining the shelves behind the counter. All were filled with lotions and potions in dazzling shades of indigo, green, violet, and orange.

"Well, how can I help you?"

A bespectacled man with a shaggy beard enquired.

"I am expecting a baby in the autumn, but I want something to help me with morning sickness and heartburn in the evenings."

A sense of loneliness gripped her as she realised that she was sharing her most intimate secret with a total stranger. She struggled to control the quiver in her voice, but his eyes went to her gloved hands and lingered on the left one.

"Well, can you assist me?"

He rearranged his spectacles on his nose and without another word went into a back room. Some minutes later he returned with two small brown bottles.

Pointing to them he said.

"This one with the green top is to prevent retching while the other one is guaranteed to stop the most stubborn of heartburn. Now, that will be two shillings, please. "

She handed him the coins and he put the bottles surreptitiously into a brown paper bag which he placed on the counter. When she reached for them, he grabbed her left hand and felt beneath the kid leather.

"Just as I thought! No ring! I can tell your kind a mile off. You are not a married woman."

She snatched her hand away from him.

"How dare you! I can swear on my baby's life that I am a married woman, but my fingers are inclined to swell so I took the ring off this morning, besides it's not your business."

He sniggered.

"That's what they all say. Believe you me, I have heard every excuse under the sun from women like yourself. Look, I don't care about your morals but for a few pounds, I can offer you the name of a good nurse who will get rid of that thing in your belly. Sure, it's great fun when a man pokes you but not so good when you have to suffer the consequences."

Shaking with a mixture of rage and embarrassment, Sarah grabbed the bag off the counter as she rebuked him.

"You are nothing but a dirty, unscrupulous man who is trying to make money from other people's misfortune. I thank God that I am married and that I want to keep my baby, but God help any unmarried girl who ends up in trouble and finds herself in your clutches."

"You know where to find me if you change your mind!"

He called, as she opened the door and stepped outside.

She paused for a moment to arrange her thoughts and calm her nerves, while he followed her to the entrance and called after her for all the street to hear.

"Get out of here, you are a filthy whore."

With crimson cheeks and her head bowed she ducked into a nearby lane which led to a warren of side streets. Picking her way carefully to avoid heaps of horse manure, rotting vegetables and open sewerage pipes she eventually reached the end of them and emerged onto Lord Edward Street. Still in shock from her encounter with the chemist, she walked quickly without stopping to check for directions. For a moment she thought she was lost and then she worked out that she was on Dame street as the huge stone fort of Dublin Castle loomed out of the smoke. Her heart seemed to beat louder as she approached.

It was the headquarters of British rule in Ireland, from here the Lord Lieutenant and the Chief Secretary ruled the whole island. She had heard Sean say that the newly appointed Chief Secretary Ian Macpherson was a man of hubris with no regard whatsoever for the Irish.

She smiled to herself as she imagined how they would react if they knew that at that very moment the wife of one of the most wanted men in the country was on their doorstep.

She had scarcely passed the main gates when a commotion behind her made her stop and turn around. Two Crossley tenders carrying members of the Dublin Metropolitan Police drove out noisily through the massive gates onto the street followed by a Crossley truck carrying several armed men in mismatched uniforms who were roaring at the top of their voices. She guessed that these must be the

Reserves, who according to the newspapers were rapidly earning a reputation for brutality as well as the nickname *Black and Tans.*

One of them shouted something at her as they passed but amid all the din, she could not tell what it was. She noted that pedestrians were quickly scurrying in every direction down alleyways and into doorways, to get out of sight of the dreaded new recruits.

A ragged woman with a pram full of apples abandoned them and shouted to Sarah to take cover with her.

"Get down before they start shooting."

Sarah copied her and they crouched in the doorway of a nearby shop.

Then the sound of vehicles screeching to a halt followed by gunfire echoed through the deserted streets.

From her military drilling, Sarah reckoned that they were using pump-action shotguns and automatic pistols.

There were ear-splitting shouts followed by more commands.

Then the unmistakable revving of engines as they roared off in the direction of the city centre.

Then an eerie silence.

Nothing stirred, even the family of young rats in a nearby drain who had been squealing moments earlier were silent.

At least five minutes passed before a clear, high pitched whistle sounded from the far recesses of the street and then there was bedlam.

Men and women ran frantically to aid the dying and wounded.

Sarah, peering in the direction of the bloodshed felt suddenly sick and emptied the contents of her stomach onto the street. In other circumstances, she would not have hesitated to help but given that she was pregnant and nauseous she decided to take the advice of the apple seller.

"Go home love, this is no place for the faint-hearted."

A man from a nearby bakery, running with a bundle of flour bags under his arm called to the woman.

"Sally can you give us a hand, I am going to make bandages out of these bags to stop the bleeding. There are several wounded, those fuckers were looking for Patsey Riordan and when they could not find him, they shot at passers-by."

Sarah watched as the woman gathered her shawl around her shoulders and ran after him down the street. Sean had mentioned Patsey Riordan in connection with the shooting dead of a magistrate in Kildare the previous year. Suddenly, she felt goose pimples all over her body and she half-walked half-ran all the way back to Capel Street where she got on a tram to the railway station.

The following day, Rita with characteristic disregard for her own safety and despite Sarah's warning about not visiting until things settled down, dropped in and insisted on cooking a full meal. Afterwards, she remarked.

"You look a little peaky, I hope that you are not coming down with something."

Sarah met her gaze and shrugged off the suggestion.

"Not at all. I feel great. It's probably just delayed shock from all I witnessed yesterday. Let me tell you about it, now that we have finished that delicious food."

Rita sat on the edge of her chair.

"The papers say a man and woman died on the spot and up to 12 people were wounded. There but for the grace of God, you could have been killed."

Sarah replied with levity.

"I am as tough as old boots!"

Then she described what she had seen while Rita hung on every word.

"I must say I am both surprised and relieved that for once you did not get involved with tending to the poor unfortunates. There was a strong possibility that those brutes would return and start shooting again."

Rita removed her spectacles and rubbed her eyes.

For a moment Sarah held her breath, she did not want to reveal the real reason for her decision to walk away.

"I suppose you think that I was cowardly but there were people running everywhere, it was sheer hell. My instinct was to get out of the area as I had only strayed onto that street by accident."

Rita reassured her.

"Look here, you were right to go. I am not judging you at all."

Sarah gave a weak smile.

"It wasn't my finest hour, turning tail like that and running but what can I say except that one never can predict how one will react in a given situation."

Rita gave her a reassuring pat on the back.

"I would have done the same myself, you were out of your depth. You were too close to that castle for comfort and those English hounds sitting in there ready to pounce!"

Sarah laughed at her choice of words and then decided to change the subject as she felt guilty about not revealing the real reason for her swift departure from that awful scene.

That night, she dreamt that she was back outside the castle and that the *Black and Tans* were pumping bullets into Sean's lifeless body. She rose early and wrote a short, coded letter to him, as it was possible that he had not received her last one. She felt hurt and abandoned that she could not share news of her pregnancy with him and it raised all her old insecurities associated with losing her own mother at a young age and being abandoned by her father. Then, for a long time, she agonised about telling Rita, but she decided that it was better to keep it to herself. She did not want Rita fussing and worse still, moving in with her as it might only draw unwanted attention on them both.

On Thursday, Sarah cycled into the village after school. At the local whist drive the previous evening she had heard gossip about Mel Geraghty. And she wanted to check if the rumours were true. She had just dismounted from her bicycle when Terence Flynn pulled up beside her in his gleaming motor car and got out.

Removing his hat, he said.

"Good afternoon Miss Murphy. I trust that you are keeping well."

"Good afternoon to you Mr Flynn. Yes, I am well, thank you."

She turned to go but he said in a low voice.

"Have you heard about Geraghty and his drunken rantings?"

She looked directly at him.

"Just rumours but it is really not my business."

He responded.

"Perhaps you should make it your business. You see he drank a full bottle of whiskey on Saturday and paid a visit to everyone who was ever kind to Eamonn, even in the smallest way."

Sarah shrugged. "Why?"

He gestured in the direction of the barber's shop.

"The fool is enraged that his son ran away and feels that he has to blame someone else. He cannot just accept that the boy had enough brains between his ears to go of his own accord."

Raising an eyebrow, Sarah enquired.

"Did he approach you?"

"He followed me into Brennan's bar and threatened to knife me if I did not admit to driving Eamonn into Dublin and getting him a job in one of the big stores."

"Had you any dealings with the boy?"

Sarah enquired, as she tried to keep her expression calm.

He ran his fingers through his greasy hair.

"About one week before Eamonn left, I paid him to wash and polish my motor. He did such a good job that I gave him a spin in it afterwards, the poor lad was delighted.

I promised that I would give him the job again but then he disappeared a few days later."

Sarah gave a glib reply.

"The father is as mad as a hatter and too fond of the whiskey."

He looked at her for a moment.

"I am surprised that he did not call on you as I believe Eamonn attended your evening classes."

Sarah conceded.

"Yes, Eamonn was a good student, but I was in Dublin on Saturday so I cannot say if that lunatic came to my house looking for me."

He let out a low whistle.

"I just wanted to put you on your guard as he has at least five or six people on a blacklist and he has approached all of them, except you and the magistrate."

"Do you mean William Taylor?" Sarah asked, trying to suppress her surprise.

Terence Flynn grimaced.

"Yes, he is a harmless old fool. They say he spends most of his free time drinking or gambling. Apparently, he gave a threepenny bit one day to Eamonn for retrieving his hat which a gust of wind had swept from his head - he was on his way into the courthouse at the time."

Sarah laughed.

"It's crazy! So, he suspects that the magistrate encouraged Eamonn to leave home. I doubt it, someone of his stature is too wily to get involved at that level."

"Ah, true! But I wanted you to know about his antics! Forewarned is forearmed! I take it you were meeting your sweetheart in Dublin but forgive me, it is not my business. I have a lady friend myself now and so all's well that ends well."

Sarah gave an affirmatory nod of her head.

"Thank you so much Mr Flynn for your concern. I am glad to hear that you have found love again and I hope that you will be very happy together."

Flattered, he gave a high-pitched laugh.

"Thank you, Miss Murphy, now I must be on my way."

It was later that evening when she took out her Webley Revolver and cleaned it thoroughly. Next, she practised loading it quickly as she knew that in a real emergency a minute or two could mean the difference between life and death. Now that she was expecting a baby, she had to make sure that she had taken every precaution to defend her life and that of her unborn child if Geraghty turned up with a knife.

She patted her stomach and spoke softly.

"My little darling, what sort of a life will you have with all this turmoil going on in the background? And will you end up like me, never knowing your daddy?"

She made a mug of hot milk with a few drops of whiskey and nutmeg thrown in for good measure. Then she carried it to her bedroom where she adjusted the telescope until it brought the stars into full view. Somewhere under that same sky, she took comfort in imagining what Sean was doing at that very minute.

Chapter Twelve

As Sarah left the church that Sunday after midday mass, she noticed Mel Geraghty lingering in the graveyard near some old tombstones. She had stayed behind to light candles, the dark interior of the solemn Victorian building resonating with her own fears about Sean's safety.

When she approached him, she noticed a stack of books in his arms which she instantly recognised as belonging to her. She had left them in a hiding place at the well for Eamonn as she had promised after he was prohibited from attending her evening classes.

"Miss Murphy, I have books here with your name written in bold print on them so do not deny that they are yours."

Sarah remained outwardly calm but her heart was beating faster than normal.

"Where did you get them?"

He waved one hand in the air.

"Don't play the innocent with me! I found them only last night hidden under old hay in the byre, Eamonn must have buried them there because he knew how I felt about you and your book-learning."

"Well, thank you so much for returning them to me, I am grateful."

Her voice was modulated.

He stuck his neck out like a turkey cock and shouted.

"You think that you are so clever! Enticing my boy to greener pastures! And filling his head with lies about being overworked in the forge. Where did you send him?"

"It's a funny thing," reflected Sarah. "That you are blaming me and everyone else in the area who was kind to Eamonn, for his departure. Can you not see that the boy has a mind of his own?"

"You bitch."

She ignored him and continued.

"Let's face it, even the dogs in the street know that you almost killed him after your nephew drowned in the lake."

He edged closer to her and dropped the books at her feet.

"I can see in your eyes that you are not telling the truth. And one way or another I will get to the bottom of your lies."

Sarah returned his stare.

"Look, he is a great young man, you should be proud of him. Why don't you just get on with your life and let the matter rest? You cannot continue making a fool of your-self by accusing people left right and centre of leading him astray."

She stooped to pick up the books, but he stood delib-erately on her right foot.

Wincing with pain she cried.

"Stop! Remove your foot at once."

But he pressed even harder and she screamed at the top of her voice.

"You bastard!"

From the small door at the side of the church, an altar boy came running followed by Fr. Daly.

"What on earth is going on?" He enquired.

Geraghty answered in honeyed tones.

"Nothing at all, I was just helping the schoolteacher pick up her books when I accidentally stood on her foot, it was an accident, but she started screaming like a madwoman!"

The priest looked from one to another.

"Is this true Miss Murphy?"

Taking a step backwards, she never took her eyes off her assailant.

"It's all lies, this man would not know the truth if it tapped him on the shoulder."

Fr. Daly clenched his knuckles in disgust.

"Miss Murphy, we all make mistakes. Can you not just forgive him?"

Sarah protested.

"This was a deliberate act of violence against my person."

Mel Geraghty adopted an avuncular pose.

"I really am sorry for the mishap. Perhaps, Fr. Daly you will make this good lady see sense."

The priest exploded.

"I have to attend to my flock. Two adults fighting like cocks!"

Sarah, who was filled with rage, struggled to find the right words.

She opened her mouth and promptly closed it again.

Meanwhile, Geraghty proceeded to roar with laughter.

"The whole parish knows how generous I have been to widows who are down on their luck. How could this woman even think that I planned to hurt her by standing on her foot?"

Suddenly, Fr. Daly looked from one to the other and commanded.

"Leave this cemetery now! I will not tolerate either of you disrespecting the dead. This is a place of peace!"

Under his watchful eye, Sarah picked up her books and limped over to the wall where she had propped her bicycle while her accuser stormed off down the street muttering to himself.

By the time she came to the bend in the road, she had banished all thoughts of him as her senses took in the glorious spring day. Cycling slowly, a medley of birdsong from the trees and hedgerows filled her ears while an endless display of primroses and cowslips on banks and ditches caught her eye. Yet, it was the heady aroma of coconut from the furze bushes which filled her with delight and made her want to burst into song.

However, in a matter of minutes, her mood changed again when she caught sight of a Ford Model T motor car parked in front of her gate. By the time she reached it a slim man in a chauffeur's uniform had alighted and extended his hand to her.

"Miss Murphy, please allow me to introduce myself. I am Jack Finnegan, Adjutant of the 2nd Battalion Dublin North, I have been asked to escort you to a meeting."

She noted his gravelly voice but ignored his offer of a handshake while she settled her bicycle against the hedge. Then turning to him she said in a firm voice.

"You seem to have made a mistake, I have no idea who sent you, but I think that you should enquire in the first public house on the left-hand side of the village and the proprietor will direct you to your destination."

He smiled with a touch of conceit.

"I have made no mistake, let me use the password and you will see that I know what I am doing; *Amergin.*"

She gasped it was one of the passwords used by a handful of men who worked closely with Sean in the IRA.

"Who sent you? And why are you dressed in that ridiculous uniform?"

He guffawed.

"I wish you had to wear it as it's not comfortable but it's part of my disguise in case we encounter any of his Majesty's forces."

He spat on the ground to show his revulsion for them and then continued.

"I can say that I am driving you back to the city after a visit to your cousin Lady Fingal. I have a swanky hat and coat for you to wear and some false papers as well if they stop us. I am delighted to make your acquaintance Lady Mary Seymour."

He touched his cap in a mock show of deference.

Still wary of him she declared.

"I will need something more than a single word in Irish before I journey into the night with a strange man."

He removed his peaked hat and showed her a letter which he had concealed under it.

"Have a look at that handwriting." His eyes narrowed.

Immediately, she recognised it as her own and that it was the last letter which she had sent to Sean.

"This still proves nothing, for all I know you could be from the castle! It has been opened."

He lowered his voice.

"Mr Collins or Michael if you wish wants to talk with you and if I were in your shoes, I would do as he asks. I am told he met Sean in a certain prison camp across the water and together they played rings around those above them. Now, can you hurry up please?"

She stiffened at the mention of Sean and the oblique reference to his prison activities at Frongoch.

"Will Sean be with Mick Collins?"

She asked, convinced at last that this man in the chauffeur's uniform was genuine.

He shook his head.

"Don't ask me, I am only the messenger. Mick Collins is the boss, and he does not tell me what's going on in that mind of his. All I know is that he is one wily Cork man and that we are lucky to have him as he can outwit the pompous buffoons in the castle every time."

Checking the old dusty road in both directions and satisfied that it was clear apart from Tom Rafferty's skinny cow which was grazing the long acre, she spoke in a voice choking with emotion.

"Give me five minutes to change into these clothes, the quicker we get out of here the better. I don't want my elderly neighbour Willie Downey spotting me in these fine clothes as it will only arouse their curiosity."

He reached for a packet of cigarettes in his pocket.

"You are lucky that he lives near the bend in the road as he won't see much from here, now time is of the essence, Miss Murphy."

While she changed into the purple silk dress with matching jacket and flamboyant hat she wondered if the chauffeur called Jack Finnegan knew that she had married Sean in a secret ceremony. And her ears buzzed as she tried not to dwell on the purpose of this meeting with Mick Collins. The Big Fellow as his friends called him, had been recently appointed Minister for Finance by the self-styled first Irish government or Dail, with Cathal Brugha as the President.

Sitting in the back of the motor car she gripped the top of the driver's seat nervously as they encountered a motley number of horse and ass drawn carts, piled with everything from animal dung to hay and turf. Darkness had fallen by the time they arrived at the ruins of an old Abbey deep in the countryside of Kildare. They had spent the previous couple of hours bypassing the main roads to avoid officers of the crown, rattling over bog roads and across lanes that were little more than dirt tracks. Several times the driver was forced to stop and get out with a spade and shovel to clear a route through flooded mucky trails.

And each time he did so Sarah jumped out and inhaled great gulps of fresh air as she feared that her stomach might decide to empty itself at any moment. Miraculously she did not vomit in his car but when it finally came to a shuddering halt near the towering wall of a Cistercian Abbey she threw up everything which she had eaten that day.

"I am so sorry about the journey, it was a rough drive," Jack declared as he offered her a sip of whiskey from a Power's bottle.

She declined saying, "Don't mind me, it's not your fault, I have a weak stomach at the best of times. Now, where is Mr Collins?"

Throwing back his head he laughed.

"We have another bit to go yet, as you know Mick is a wanted man like Sean, so we have to be careful in case someone followed us here."

For a long time, they stood in silence while the screeches of nocturnal animals echoed through the ruins and caused shivers to run up Sarah's spine. Eventually, an ass and cart materialised out of the darkness and they climbed on board behind a little old woman who exchanged a greeting with

Jack in Irish. It took another ten minutes through bogland before they pulled up beside a deserted farmhouse with slates missing from the roof, and at least a half a mile from the nearest lane.

"At last!"

Jack declared while he helped her get down from the cart.

"You cannot be serious! There is no one here."

Suddenly, she felt dizzy, as a sense of panic gripped her, and she wondered if it was all a trap by rogue members of Sinn Fein who were intent on reaching Sean through her.

"I am not going one step further until-." Her voice grew faint.

"Please don't despair, Miss Murphy, have faith."

He waved at the old woman who turned the pony and trap around and disappeared into the night.

Then he cleared his throat.

"When your eyes grow accustomed to the darkness you will see that there is an old hay barn behind the trees. Follow me."

She picked her way through the undergrowth in the paper-thin purple shoes and then around to the back of the barn. When she raised her eyes from ground level, in the moonlight she saw the outline of a low building with a thatch roof and a glimmer of light in the windows.

"My God! I would never have guessed that this dwelling was here! It's away from prying eyes."

Jack sniggered.

"It's known as the mushroom, it appeared in a matter of weeks, you see we stayed up at night last summer to build it. And we have a friend in the local barracks who turned a blind eye to our comings and goings."

"It's wonderful but is Sean here?"

She enquired as her heart seemed to pound loudly in her breast.

"Be quiet for a minute!"

He said as they approached the door. Cupping his hand, he made a series of taps on it and it opened slowly to reveal a barrel-chested man in his forties.

"Francie, let us in before this lady dies of exhaustion!"

"Jackser Finnegan! I see you have indeed brought a fine lady with you! Step inside and mind your heads!"

He doffed his cap to her as Sarah removed her flouncy hat and entered a small room with a table and four chairs.

There was evidence of a recent meal and several cigarette butts on the mud floor.

"Sit down, sit down."

The man called Francie intoned in a jocular fashion. Then, dangling a cigarette from the side of his mouth he said.

"Jackser, go out and keep watch. I will rouse the Big Fellow and tell him that this lovely lady is here at last."

Sarah sat on the edge of a chair while she tried to compose herself. Now and then sipping from a mug of frothy milk which had been placed in front of her.

Suddenly, she heard a thick Cork brogue from a nearby room as the door was flung open by a tall man with broad shoulders.

"Francie, are you losing the run of yourself with this pretty lady. Why not tell me that my guest had arrived? Or were you trying to keep her all to yourself?"

He advanced towards her with arm outstretched. In the light of the lamp, as they shook hands, she saw that he had a well-proportioned face with dancing eyes and a devilish grin. She had never seen his photograph and was taken aback by his good looks.

"Miss Murphy, I am delighted to meet you at last and please accept my apologies for dragging you through the night to this God-forsaken place."

She was aware of his eyes on hers as she replied.

"It's a great pleasure to meet with you, Mr Collins. I have heard a lot about you from Sean. You have found a wild but beautiful place to rest awhile."

He chuckled and touched her arm lightly.

"We can talk in comfort in my den please follow me. And Francie could you make us a cup of tea along with some of the roast chicken and brown bread your good wife sent to me?"

"No problem at all Mick, give me a while until I get the kettle boiling."

His room was a cross between an office and a bed-room. On one side books and newspapers were stacked up in piles against the walls while on the other side she saw a make-shift bed covered with woollen blankets next to a wash-stand which held a basin and a large jug of water. In the centre of the floor, a table which doubled as a desk was strewn with maps and several hand-written letters. Two old wooden chairs stood beside it and she was relieved when he invited her to sit on one of them as the strain of the journey was beginning to tell on her back. He sat opposite and poured generous measures of brandy into two glasses. Then handing her one he said.

"To Sean."

While he drank the contents in a couple of mouthfuls, she took measured sips from hers.

Unable to bear the suspense any longer she asked with tremulous hands.

"Where is Sean? Will he be joining us?"

For a few awful minutes, there was absolute silence as she heard the distinctive sound of a fox howling from the bog. Then he leaned forward across the desk and she noticed his full, generous lips.

"That is the reason for bringing you here, I am sorry to tell you that our last contact with him was on the twenty-second day of January but before you jump to any conclusions, it does not necessarily mean that he is dead. There are several possible reasons why he has not been seen."

She saw the papers on the desk swimming before her eyes and she gripped the edge of her chair while she heard him say.

"Miss Murphy, you don't look at all well!"

She took out a hankie from her handbag and wiped her forehead, where beads of sweat were threatening to drop into her eyes. Then, finishing the remainder of the brandy in her glass she sat poker straight in her chair, hiding her hands which were shaking, under her long sleeves.

"Yes, I am fine. I just got a shock, that's all."

She felt the golden liquid warm her insides while she recovered control of her body.

"This is the news which I have always feared but as you say there may be a reasonable explanation for his absence."

Mick Collins rubbed the stubble on his chin with his left hand and then spoke in a gentle voice.

"Please allow me to call you Mrs Byrne, now that we are in a safe place, the time has come for total honesty between us."

She pursed her lips in agreement.

"Forget formalities, just call me Sarah."

"Ok Sarah, so you must call me Mick, everyone else does apart from the Brits! Only God knows the title they have on me."

She tried to smile at his joke and then fidgeted with the buttons on her sleeve as she spoke. "Mick, I am begging you to tell me everything you know about Sean."

His face was full of compassion.

"I have at least 5 individuals working fulltime on it, we have Intelligence cells all over the country."

She asked in a croaky voice.

"In your own opinion, what do you think happened to him?"

He pushed back his chair and stretched out his long legs.

"God alone knows that answer because all I can do is guess as to his fate. He may have been captured by either the crown forces or by a splinter group within our own organisation. There was trouble between his group, and one created by a troublemaker called Brennan."

"I know. It was an ugly, nasty business," she ventured

"Well, either group could be holding him as a prisoner and planning to force us to give in to their demands."

He paused, took out a packet of cigarettes and offered her one.

She dismissed it with a wave of her hand.

"They could have just killed him!"

He looked closely at her.

"Indeed, but usually our men on the ground would hear about it, there are ways of making people talk. He was last seen leaving a safe house near Multyfarnham, in Westmeath. The plan was that he would cut across fields and follow the river until he came to a certain landmark - one of our lads was waiting to bring him to a local meeting which he planned to address, but he never showed up."

A deep wail escaped from her chest.

"The whole countryside is crawling with Black and Tans not to mention RIC men!"

He agreed.

"Yes, but if they just shot him it is likely that someone would hear about it, we have our spies as they have theirs. Money loosens the tongue whether you are Irish or English. I have to say Sarah that the longer this continues..."

Her voice was filled with fear.

"I am not stupid Mick I know that as each day passes the chances of finding him alive grow slimmer."

His face reddened.

"If he is dead it may be due to some natural cause, he may have slipped on the bank and fallen into the river, the currents at this time of the year are especially strong."

She emptied the last dregs from her glass and banged the table with her fist.

"You know the cruellest thing about all of this is the uncertainty. Questions arise in my mind day and night, sometimes even when I am dreaming.

Is he dead?

Is he alive?

Is he being held captive?

Is he being tortured?

Is he lying at the bottom of a bog hole or a lake?

Is he buried like a pauper in some unmarked grave? It's enough to drive anyone mad!"

Mick stood up and came around to her side of the desk. Then very gently he laid a hand on her shoulder.

"Sarah, I want you to know that I look on Sean as a brother and that I will do everything possible to get answers for you."

She looked up into his tender eyes and at that moment she knew that Mick Collins believed that Sean was dead, but he was trying to break it to her gently.

A soft tap on the door interrupted their conversation.

Mick returned to his chair and said in a teasing tone.

"Come in Francis! We are starving! Did you have to kill the chicken first!"

Sarah dried her eyes and moved to the tiny window while the desk was cleared and prepared for the meal. For a few moments, she wondered if it could all just be a nightmare and in a few minutes she would she wake up snug in her own bed where all was well. Then, Mick placed a firm hand on her arm and guided her towards the table.

"Please, my dear lady, eat something, I am so sorry that I have nothing positive to tell you at this stage."

One hour had passed since she sat down with Michael Collins to eat.

In different circumstances, she would have revelled in his company and his anecdotes about growing up in rural Cork. There was no doubt about his charisma and his friendly, passionate voice which made her feel as if he had no other worries apart from Sean's disappearance.

Yet, her heart was broken, and she wanted to be alone, far away from everyone where she was free to scream and rail against a God who would allow this to happen.

Just when she had fallen pregnant with Sean's baby he had been snatched from her. And now it seemed that he would never even know that he had a child on the way.

Mick coughed discreetly and joked.

"A penny for your thoughts! I only wish that I had better news, but I wanted to tell you face to face."

She managed a tight smile.

"I appreciate the effort involved in setting up this meeting."

He took out a white envelope from his waistcoat pocket and placed it in her hand.

"Please, accept this small token, it is just my way of saying that I am not just paying lip-service to Sean's disappearance. Words cannot express how upset I am as we first met at Frongach, or as Sean would say 'the university across the pond'."

She protested but he insisted.

"If you don't need it, at least spend it on your pupils to make life easier for them."

"Thank you so much for thinking of them."

Suddenly, a desire to throw herself into his arms and be comforted by his broad shoulders and soothing voice possessed her. However, the logical side of her brain sent her a warning message.

"Your hormones are all over the place! Do not cross a line and disgrace *yourself in front of this attractive, kind man!"*

She took out a handkerchief and blew her nose hard. The moment passed and she heard Mick say.

"Be assured Sarah that as soon as I hear anything which might shed light on Sean's whereabouts, I will send one of the lads to you. In the meantime, we must hope for the best but -."

She finished his sentence, "But be prepared for the worst."

Silence filled the space between them.

Then she spoke.

"I cannot help but recall Shakespeare's words; as flies to wanton boys, are we to the gods; they kill us for their sport."

"Well spoken."

He replied as she noticed the sad look in his eyes. Then the sound of a donkey braying made her jump and he peered out the window.

"Your chariot awaits! Maggie will take you and Jack back to the old Abbey, from there he will drive you home. Take care Sarah and remember if you need help do not hesitate in contacting the Mulroys of Prussia Street, you can trust those sisters with your life."

She bit her lip because she did not want to break down in front of this charming man.

"Thank you, Mick. I know that you have many people tugging at your sleeve. So, I am glad you have found this bolt hole where you can find peace now and again."

He gave her a big grin which reminded her of a naughty schoolboy who had just been caught copying from the pupil beside him.

He stood beside her and held open his long arms. They hugged for a moment and she was aware of his puppy dog eyes and a spicy scent of aftershave lotion.

Then Jack knocked loudly and opened the door.

"Mick it's time for us to go."

She exchanged a knowing look with Mick and followed the driver outside.

It was almost daybreak and high up in the ash trees birds were already singing. For a few seconds, she stood and took in the beauty of this remote place, reminding herself that it was most unlikely she would ever be there again.

"Miss Murphy, we have to leave - now, it's a long journey back." Jack's voice was steely.

"I know. I know."

He helped her up into the dusty cart and they took off at a steady pace. The old woman spoke to him in Irish while she spent that journey ruminating on the nature of existence. And how her life seemed to have changed so much in the few hours since leaving her cottage to meet with Mick Collins.

A tiny voice in her brain prompted her.

For all intents and purposes, it looks like you are a widow!

The sentence rattled around in her head as the wheels of the cart went around and around.

Chapter Thirteen

By the time Sarah arrived home, it was past midday, changing into her own clothes she peddled recklessly in the direction of the school. She had been so engrossed in her own troubles that she had totally forgotten about her pupils.

From several yards away she heard the sing- voices of the children chanting the seven deadly sins as stated in the old brown catechism.

Inside, Fr. Daly was ensconced in her chair smoking a pipe.

When she opened the door, a hush fell on the room and he exclaimed in mock surprise.

"Miss Murphy! I am so glad to see that you are still in the land of the living!"

Flustered, she wiped her brow while she concocted an excuse.

"Fr. Daly, I am so sorry, my second cousin once removed is home from America, she sent a motor car and chauffeur to collect me and take me to the Shelbourne Hotel where she is staying, she married a rich yank."

His face was thunderous

"I am appalled that you just swanned off and did not tell me. It was Mrs Kelly who informed me that the pupils were running wild around the schoolyard like goats!"

"I am truly sorry, I thought that I would be home in time to open the school. Please, forgive me, it won't happen again."

He harrumphed.

"This is the second time you have made a disgrace of yourself and if it happens again there will be serious repercussions!"

Glancing nervously at her pupils she assured him.

"It won't happen again."

Then a thought struck her which she knew would help to dissipate his anger.

"Fr. Daly, I need to speak to you in private."

"Put those heads down and learn from your lessons!"

He snapped at the class and then strode to the back of the room where she joined him.

"My cousin gave me a generous donation to be used on my pupils and I would welcome your suggestions."

His face softened.

"In that case, I shall not take the matter of your absence any further. The McGovern family are in dire straits, Annie the mother, has consumption and if something is not done about the broken-down door and draughty windows, the whole family will perish."

She did some mental arithmetic and was satisfied that there would still be some money left over from the sum Michael Collins had given her.

"Fr. Daly, I will leave the money with your housekeeper tomorrow afternoon as I trust that you will arrange the necessary renovations."

"Indeed, be assured that the money is going to a good cause."

She nodded.

"I know, I have three from that family in the school and they are lovely little girls. Also, it is my intention to arrange with Sonny Brannigan, the cobbler, to make shoes for all my pupils, with the few pounds left from the donation, so that they won't have to walk to school barefooted in bad weather."

His eyes widened.

"Thousands of children all over the country go to school every day in bare feet, I did not own a pair of shoes until I won a scholarship to St. Vincent's Classical school for boys. Besides, children grow out of shoes quickly."

She could feel rage boiling up as an interior voice warned her.

There is no pleasing this tyrant.

She stood up straight and looked him in the eye.

"My mind is made up! It is also a way of providing extra income to the Brannigan family. They have five children under school-going age, and all are sickly and need proper medical care."

His face coloured to a deep crimson as his mood changed, and he realised that she had the upper hand for once.

"My flock have many needs and it is my duty to attend to them, to think that I was standing here like a nursemaid doing your work all morning, it is not good enough."

He strode towards the door as a young boy ran to open it for him.

She said smoothly.

"Fr. Daly, thank you again for everything, it was remiss of me, in fairness I have been an exemplary teacher otherwise."

"Good day to you!"

He patted the child on the head, leaving a trail of tobacco smoke behind him as he puffed angrily on his pipe.

Sarah shivered, every morning, apart from a few scorching days, pupils from the senior classes took it in turns to light a fire in the old red brick fireplace. The parents who could afford it send in baskets of turf and logs, while the poorer ones contributed by providing bunches of sticks and small pieces of wood for kindling. This morning without a glow from the hearth the room was chilly. She looked around at her pupils, their young faces clearly showing that they were pleased to have her back in place of the crusty priest, who was well known for using an old leather strap on boys and girls who did not know their catechism off by heart.

On Friday afternoon Rita arrived by hackney with a large grey trunk.

She laughed at Sarah's face which showed surprise.

"Don't worry, I am not moving in with you! I am on my way to Belfast, I got a telegram from my niece yesterday."

Sarah wrinkled her brow.

"Is something wrong with your niece Mary?"

"Yes. The poor soul has consumption and her husband cannot mind eight children and hold onto a job. I am going to help out as they don't want to separate the children and send them to different relatives scattered around the country."

"I am so sorry to hear that she is sick, at least two of my pupils have lost a parent in the last year to that dreaded disease." Sarah reflected.

"Mary is only thirty years old and with a young family, it seems so cruel that she has been struck down. I want to help in a practical way rather than just paying lip-service to her plight."

"You are so kind and generous." Sarah hugged her tightly.

Rita extricated herself from the embrace.

"You nearly choked me!" She said with a smile. "Now, I want to hear all about you. I am planning on spending the night here and going by train tomorrow to Belfast."

"That's the best news I have heard in a long time." Sarah said as she started to lay the table for the evening meal.

They talked for hours; about the mystery of Sean's whereabouts and her meeting with Michael Collins. Rita was perturbed that she was going away at such a difficult time and made Sarah promise to write weekly letters to her.

However, Sarah was careful not to reveal that she was with child because she did not wish to compound Rita's guilt about leaving. She had started to have crazes for certain foods including hard-boiled eggs and she had to restrain herself from eating a fourth one when Rita joked.

"My goodness, you will turn into a chicken if you eat any more eggs."

The following morning Sarah woke early. For the first few moments, everything seemed fine then it all flooded back to her; her beloved Sean was missing and now dear Rita her confidante was going away too. She put on a brave front for Rita who had arranged for the hackney man to collect her and drive her to the railway station at Drumree.

Then torn between laughing and crying, she stood at the gate waving until the vehicle disappeared in a cloud of smoke and dust.

Once she was back inside the house, she became agitated as the gravity of her situation dawned on her. It was at times such as this that the full impact of having no father or mother to support her most hurt. She knew that she had wasted too many years on passively bemoaning her lack of close family. Now, she would do something proactive about it for a change. She would request a meeting with William Taylor. Then she would insist that he reveal all he knew about her parents, including her father's desertion of her mother.

Sometimes, when she was feeling low, she saw herself as teetering on the edge of madness, between damaged and delusional. Resembling those protagonists in the Victorian novels which she had found when clearing out her grandmother's belongings after her death.

She knew too that her greatest strength of being fiercely independent was also her greatest weakness. Now, when she most needed someone to be there for her, she had no one. Apart from Maddie, she had lost touch with her old friends in Dublin and she had avoided getting close to anyone locally because of the double life which she was leading.

Given that she was about to bring another little person into the world she had to try and reach beyond her own neediness and build a stable life for the child, with or without Sean.

A voice in her head reminded her.

You don't want the child cursing their very existence like I did when I was in my teens after Granny died.

Then she stroked her belly which seemed to have grown a lot in the past two weeks.

She was now wearing the tightest of corsets to keep the bump hidden in public, but it was a great relief to her to remove it every evening once she got inside the safety of her own home. She also had a voracious appetite and following a big plate of apple pie and hot custard she lay on the bed for a rest.

It was late afternoon when she awoke, feeling more troubled than ever. Since he disappeared, Sean's tortured face haunted her in dreams. Always, the same recurring one in which he was burned at the stake, while onlookers in medieval clothing taunted him.

Reaching for the bottle of whiskey she took three swigs from it until the fear had left her body. Then she rummaged through a press and found her best writing paper and envelopes. Taking a red fountain pen and a bottle of black ink she sat at the kitchen table and proceeded to write two letters.

The first was brief and addressed to The Right Honourable William Taylor, requesting a meeting with him. While the second was long and rambling, addressed to Maddie in London. She had not heard from her friend since Christmas when a hastily scrawled card arrived. Maddie was staying near Oxford, nursing some high-ranking officer through his last illness. Sarah wrote about her fears for Sean's life and her meeting with Michael Collins.

And then in the final paragraph, she revealed that she was with child and intended to stay with Maddie in London once school finished in June.

Blessing herself, she sealed both letters and placed them in her handbag.

Her first task the next day was to stick stamps, showing the king's head, on each letter and then she dropped them into the red letterbox outside the post office. Although it was a Sunday which meant that the letters would remain overnight in the box she did not dare hold onto them until the following morning in case she changed her mind and decided to burn them.

The sarcastic voice in her head said.

God knows you have agonised for days about writing them.

However, to drown out the words, she hummed to herself as she walked away from the letterbox, almost colliding with a group of children who appeared from around a corner as they chased a brown dog who was carrying a string of sausages in his mouth.

Some of them were her pupils but she refrained from chastising them.

"Sorry Miss, Bonny stole our dinner!"

Colm, the eldest boy, shouted.

She stood for a few minutes watching them as they gave chase to the dog who was intent on holding onto his spoils.

Then it seemed that a giggle began in her belly and by the time it reached her mouth, she roared with laughter, while an old tramp known as "Red-faced Johnny", approached, and joined in the mirth, seizing the opportunity to get some sympathy from Sarah.

When she had regained her composure, she dug out a few halfpennies for the man, who promptly said.

"The Lord save you Miss and send a decent man to you, who will put a ring on your finger and a child in your belly."

"Away with you! I don't want to hear your dirty talk!"

She admonished him with a thunderous look.

He slunk away like a scalded cat, making her laugh all over again.

The two weeks following, brought unseasonal weather for April with low temperatures by night and heavy rainfall by day. That year was extraordinary, with First Communion and Confirmation ceremonies to be performed in the same week during the Lenten season, which meant an extra workload for Sarah because nearby parishes joined together for the sacraments. Due to an outbreak of Spanish flu in the previous autumn near the Bishop's palace, he had cancelled all his usual commitments but now he was eager to avoid a big backlog.

Later, at a special meal in the Parochial house hosted by Fr. Daly for the local bishop, she sat at a side table between two schoolmasters whose only topic of conversation concerned the possible winner of the forthcoming Grand National to be held in Fairyhouse on Easter Monday. As soon as it was acceptable, she excused herself from their company and took a stroll in the garden which was a blaze of yellow and purple. To her surprise, she was joined by the bishop and his assistant, a deacon from Maynooth college, as Fr. Daly had been summoned next door to administer the last rites to an old man in his final agony.

The bishop, swathed in a purple cassock and purple biretta, to reflect sorrow and suffering in keeping with the season of lent, walked towards her. Then lifting his right hand which had an ornate ring on the third finger to symbolise his total commitment to the Roman Catholic church, he held it out for Sarah to kiss. Furious that he expected her to fawn over him a second time as she had earlier kissed it in the church in a public display of allegiance along with her peers, she hesitated and instead shook his hand firmly.

"Your Excellency, how nice to see you outside enjoying the flowers."

His eyes narrowed at the rebuff as he withdrew his hand hurriedly

"Such impertinence! Refusing to kiss the very symbol that links me to Christ."

Sarah was about to relinquish her stance when she looked into his eyes and saw them full of hubris. Fuelled by her own fears about Sean and the fact that she would have to leave this parish forever in a matter of months because of her pregnancy, she retreated a few steps. She detested all the pomp and ceremony associated with the so-called Princes of the church and their power over the common people, who were afraid to think for themselves.

Aware that he was about to explode with rage, she said.

"My apologies, your excellency, I meant no disrespect."

"You are no better than those hypocrites in the new testament!"

He exclaimed as he adjusted his biretta and strode off without another word while his assistant shook his head in disbelief and hurried to keep up with his superior.

That evening, Sarah reflected on her encounter with the bishop. She knew that he would complain to Fr. Daly and request her removal from the school at the end of the school year, to allow them time to find a replacement over the summer holidays. And she smiled sardonically at her reflection in the mirror as she imagined how Fr. Daly would beg her to go cap in hand to the bishop's palace and recant of her ways. There she would be expected to beg the great man's forgiveness for her sins of disobedience, pride, and blasphemy so that she could hold onto her teaching position. For a moment she felt like a fool from some Elizabethan court, subject to the vagaries of those in power. Fr. Daly, so in awe of his superiors, would be appalled when she told him that she had no intention of going anywhere near the bishop's palace and that she was happy to leave. She looked forward to that exchange when she would take delight in giving a metaphorical two fingers to the males who dominated the church and ruled like despots.

For a long time, she had paid lip-service to those hierarchies whilst secretly revulsed that in their pursuit of power, they had lost sight of the real message of Christianity. Now, that she no longer had Sean's visits to savour, this small, rural community with its petty jealousies and narrow-minded views irritated her. Even her regular meetings with the philanthropic ladies of the parish disappointed her as she saw through their innate snobbery and their underlying abhorrence of the poor. She was tired – of Somerset, of her monotonous day to day existence, waiting and hoping against all hope, to hear that Sean was alive.

And to make matters even worse there were so few sources of amusement available to her locally, apart from card games, books, and newspapers. At least, if she were back in Dublin, she could distract herself with the theatre or a plethora of clubs and organisations which would challenge her intellectually.

Easter came and went and with it a long letter from Rita, who was struggling in her new role as foster mother to eight children. An Easter card arrived too from Maddie in Oxford with a few lines about her life there. It was clear to Sarah that her recent letter to Maddie's London address had not been forwarded to her and so she wrote another letter to her.

Every day she watched for the postman in the hope that he might bring a reply from William Taylor, but nothing arrived. Just when she had given up on hearing from him a motor car groaned and screeched one morning outside the school, before coming to a halt.

For a split second, her world seemed to turn upside down as she wondered if it was news about Sean but then she recognised the number plate as a local one. Delighted with any distraction, the children ran to the windows to see what was causing the commotion.

A boy by the name of Paddy Kelly shrieked at the top of his voice.

"It's the Black and Tans, get down on the floor."

She saw a middle-aged man in a grey uniform alight from it and walk up the path with his cap in hand.

"Paddy Kelly, stop telling lies. Children get back into your seats and do your lessons."

A light rap on the door and she opened it to reveal a different driver than the one she had encountered in the explosion when an attempt was made to blow up the magistrate's motor.

"Miss Murphy, his Honour has requested that you call to his residence tomorrow evening at seven pm sharp. I take it that you know he has moved recently and is renting the old Glebe house."

Sarah replied. "Indeed, I do!"

The driver threw back his head and laughed.

"Don't repeat this but I think he is away with the fairies! Apparently, he joined an occult society in Dublin in the hope of contacting the spirits of his dead son and wife."

The moments drifted by as Sarah digested this information.

He hesitated, waiting for a response while she felt as if time had reeled backwards as she thought of her dead mother.

He coughed.

"Will you call tomorrow evening? It's my night off, I won't be there."

"Oh - sorry, I was miles away. Yes, tell His Honour to expect me."

"Good! And remember not a word to him about what I told you!" He gave her a conspiratorial wink.

"Indeed, not a word! Your secret is safe with me. I did not get your name."

"Norbert Courtney, but most people call me Bert."

"Norbert thank you for delivering the message and safe driving."

He nodded.

"Good day to you."

She turned around and walked quickly to her table, aware that every eye in the classroom followed her. Tapping her right foot impatiently on the floor, she heard herself say:

"I want you all to go outside slowly and play. I must attend to some important business."

They trooped out into the spring sunshine and she mulled over how she might elicit information about her parents. Now, that she was about to meet him face to face she would need to have a plan, or it could all amount to nothing. Through the open door, she heard a plethora of excited screams and squeals as the children ran hither and thither. Straining harder, she heard one boy's voice rise louder than the others in a mock rallying cry while his playmates clapped and whistled.

"Like a true Irish man, I will kill every bleeding Black and Tan!"

Peering through the streaked window she confirmed that the speaker was Paddy Kelly, the boy who had mistaken the chauffeur for a soldier.

Only the previous week, his father had been badly beaten by "the Tans", on his way home from the bog with his ass and cart.

Shaking her head sadly, she discreetly patted her own baby growing inside her, while she whispered a silent prayer that they would not have to grow up without a father.

Chapter Fourteen

The following evening Sarah crunched up the gravel drive to the former Glebe house, having abandoned her bicycle under the shelter of a sprawling oak tree. After weeks of agonising over what she should do about William Taylor and his connection to her mother, finally, she was about to confront him. And now with a child of her own on the way, day by day she was more driven than ever to know about her own past. Exhausted after the uphill journey, she wiped beads of sweat from her brow. Then, lifting the big brass knocker on the door, she heard it echo through the silent old building while she waited and waited. After some minutes she repeated the process and sensed some movement deep within the house. Eventually, the door opened, and a black labrador burst out and sniffed her shoes and skirt, forcing her to fend him off with her handbag. Raising her eyes, she met those of the magistrate, who was admonishing the dog.

"Sit! Sit down at once Duke! Otherwise, Miss Murphy will think of us as uncouth!"

The animal eyed his master and then ran outside, lifting his hind leg at a nearby camellia bush before emptying his bladder.

The magistrate made tut-tuts of disapproval.

"My apologies Miss Murphy for such awful behaviour from Duke. Do please forgive him."

She laughed.

"Of course! Your Honour, dogs must be allowed to be dogs! Thank you for agreeing to meet with me."

A fit of coughing silenced him as he waved his hand in the air. While he recovered his breath, she got a chance to study him. He was tall, at least six feet, with a fleshy face.

His eyes were an unusual shade of brown with flecks of green, while his head was bald apart from some white hair that grew in tufts at the back and sides. And he had a striking blackish-grey moustache which seemed to lend him gravitas.

She reckoned that as a young man he would have been very handsome when bedecked in a uniform from the higher ranks of the Crown forces.

"Follow me, follow me."

He led the way across the hallway and through a series of passageways until he reached a small library cum smoking room.

"Find yourself a seat, while I pour some whiskey. I am afraid we are all alone here this evening. My housekeeper and driver both take Thursday evenings off. It is hard now to get reliable help."

She eased herself into a small sofa, adjusting the cushions while he poured honey-coloured liquid from a crystal decanter into two glasses.

"I have been battling a cough for over a week, my doctor tells me that I don't look after my health but I think that's all nonsense. This is good for clearing the windpipes!"

He quipped as he handed a glass to Sarah.

"Thank you, Your Honour."

She sipped the alcohol slowly while he sat in a high-backed chair directly facing her. Then he made a sympathetic noise.

"No doubt, you have come to see me about one of your past pupils who is in trouble with the law. I shall do my best to help but I do hope you are not here about that awful barber and his boy. Ever since I showed some kindness to young Eamonn, his father has had it in for me!"

Sarah was quick to answer.

"My visit has nothing at all to do with school or that family. I am here for a different reason it concerns my own past and my parents. You see, Your Honour, you knew them both as they worked for you many years ago."

He eyed her suspiciously and then sniffed.

"Can you be more explicit? I have had several people working for me in various capacities in the course of my long career."

Sarah continued.

"My mother's name was Molly Breslin, she worked in your house as a kitchen maid and later I believe as a cook. You were here in Meath as a district inspector at that time."

She paused to see his reaction, but he was undaunted.

"Name means nothing to me."

He reached for a thick cigar and lit it.

"My mother married a man called Thomas Murphy. He had a job locally as a gardener. They lived in a nearby cottage for some months after I was born but when she was expecting her second child he left for England and never returned."

She scanned his features for the slightest flicker of recognition, but his face remained blank.

She decided to carry on.

"One stormy night my mother went into premature labour and set out into the dark to seek help from her neighbours, but she stumbled and fell. They found her and the baby the next morning, both were dead."

He fixed his eyes on her with a look of impassivity and drew from his cigar.

"It is a sad story, but I have no recollection of it at all. During my long career, I have come across so many tales of woe that I cannot remember each one. Besides, I have had more than my own share of personal tragedy in recent years."

Trembling with anger she retaliated.

"Come now Your Honour, I think you can remember her well! I saw a letter you wrote when I was about two years old, to my grandmother in Dublin. You said that you had already paid out money towards my maintenance -."

Her hands were shaking, and her throat was bone dry.

Suddenly, he rose from his chair and threw a big log onto the fire, then checking his pocket watch he said.

"I am a busy man, and I cannot have you wasting my time with some yarn about my -my part in your mother's life."

Something about the way in which he stumbled over his words convinced her that he had full recollection.

She stared unflinchingly at him.

"I just want you to tell me all you know about my parents and why you felt duty-bound to pay money to Granny. It will give me some answers to all the questions which have haunted me all my life. I am relying on your decency and your impeccable good character."

Her flattery did not achieve the desired result.

"It is time Miss Murphy for you to leave, I have a mountain of work to get through this evening."

"Your Honour, might I remind you of the day I found you and your former chauffeur lying in the ditch following a motor accident. I did not turn my back and say that I was too busy. No, I hurried into the village to get help."

He stood with his back to the fire and looked beyond her at an oil painting of a fox hunt on the opposite wall.

Clearing his throat, he began in a smooth voice.

"Look here, I helped your mother out of the goodness of my own heart, but I don't want to be interrogated by you several years later. Yes, I do remember her well, she was a pretty, feisty young girl when she came to work for me."

"Please tell me more." Sarah's eyes beseeched him to go on.

He twirled the ends of his moustache.

"You see she caught the eye of my superior officer who came to stay with me and my wife one week for some fishing. Well, they had a tryst and she ended up in the family way."

Sarah could not contain herself any longer.

"What happened to that child?"

His countenance was stern as he resumed.

"My dear Miss Murphy, that child was your good self, that man was your father, but he did not want the truth to come out as he was already a married man with a family in England. Besides, it would hamper his illustrious career if word got out that he was - shall we say - overstepping himself with a local woman."

While the words rang in her ears, her cheeks burned with indignation.

"So, you are telling me that some English officer is my father!"

He rubbed his hands together.

"Yes. He was your father, but he is dead. He was sent to India and contracted some disease there, he died just a few years later."

She looked at him dubiously.

"I don't understand, what about your letter to my grandmother?"

He blew his nose before replying.

"At the time, the man in question asked me to cover it all up and provided a sum of money to make it look respectable. I knew that your mother had been courting

Thomas Murphy for some time and so I arranged for them to get married. I paid him a substantial amount of cash to say that the child on the way was his."

Sarah bit her lip, she needed to ask so many questions but did not want to interrupt him lest he refused to tell her any more about her father.

"Please, continue."

The magistrate spoke slowly as though reading from a difficult script.

"Murphy was a renegade - a scoundrel who had no regard for your mother and when she was expecting her second child, he upped and left her. He was only with her for the money and when it ran out, he fled."

Tears ran down her cheeks and she dabbed at them with her handkerchief.

"Miss Murphy, I have upset you and I apologise but you did insist on hearing the truth. Now, I really must ask you to leave, I shall see you out - the story ends there but may I say that you have turned into a lovely, smart young woman, the young men must be lining up to marry you. Any man would be proud - to be your father."

She saw him hesitate for a few seconds and his eyes narrow as if he had just recalled something else.

"What is it? Please tell me more." She pleaded.

However, he snapped his fingers in the direction of the door and without another word he strode from the room.

She followed him like a lost sheep, shocked by all he had revealed.

When they were both standing outside the big, mahogany door he turned and faced her.

"Good evening Miss Murphy."

"Your Honour, you did not give me his name." She spoke slowly.

He looked at her in shock.

"I shall never betray my friend's trust even though he is dead. Now, leave! Do you forget who I am?"

She swallowed hard and dug her nails into her wrists. She wanted to shout and hurl verbal abuse at him, but he was a man of the law, and she had to be mindful of this.

"Thank you, Your Honour."

Her legs felt unsteady and she gripped the wall. However, he had already fled into the house and closed the door with a bang that would echo in her ears for many nights to come.

In the immediate days following her visit to the Glebe, Sarah mulled over every single word that the magistrate had spoken. And when she grew tired of that exercise, she tried to work out all that had been left unsaid. She had so many questions and so few answers.

It was troubling to hear that her father was an English officer but on reflection, she was convinced that Taylor was hiding something about her real father. The more she dwelt on it the more she realised that it was a nice, convenient way to stop her in her tracks by saying that he was dead. He was saving his own skin and making sure that she would not pester him again for further information. For all she knew, her real father could be in Dublin Castle directing operations to bring about the end of the unrest and mayhem spreading across the country. And worse still he could even at this very time be overseeing officers who were keeping Sean captive in some hellhole to use him as a pawn in their game at a later stage.

Back in the schoolroom, Sarah noticed a growing restlessness spreading among her pupils. It was the same every year whether, in the city or the country, the children's concentration grew weaker and weaker with the long stretch in the evenings and the lure of three months holidays just ahead when they were free to roam as they pleased. Several of the older ones were absent from school as they were needed to work in the bog or to help with other farm chores. In the evenings she kept herself busier than ever. Firstly, by increasing the home visits which she made to the poor of the parish and secondly, by adding extra classes for her students who intended to sit for scholarship exams, to qualify for funded secondary education in nearby towns. She appreciated how important those exams were to pupils aspiring to raise themselves out of grinding poverty as she had taken a similar route herself.

Despite all this voluntary work, there was a marked coolness between her and Fr. Daly.

Ever since her run-in with the bishop, he had adopted a formal tone and conversed with her about problems strictly relating to the school. She knew that it was only a matter of time before a letter arrived from the Bishop's palace informing her that her contract at the school would cease at the end of that term.

The weekends were the worst. All alone in her cottage, time seemed interminable. Sometimes when she sought diversion through painting or reading, the ceaseless tick, tock, tick, tock, of the wall clock would become too much for her and she would rush outside to walk in the garden or across the bog, where the trilling sound of skylarks overhead never failed to bring a smile to her face. Then, she would place a loving hand on her belly and tell her baby the names of all the birds and the plants around her.

One Sunday evening when she was returning home from a whist-drive she glanced and noticed Mel Geraghty standing inside the door of Higgin's public house with a broken glass in one hand and a pint of Guinness in the other. She peddled furiously because his disembodied voice could be heard in the street as he uttered a long string of profanities. It was only when she had left the village behind and was within sight of her own cottage that she dared to slow down. In recent weeks tongues had wagged about a vicious beating which he meted out to his wife because she had not had his dinner ready on time. His constant irascibility was a cause for concern with an increasing number of his customers who choose to go elsewhere. However, he still managed to maintain a thriving business as members of the constabulary and some "Black and Tans" frequented his barber's shop not only for his skill with the scissors but to gleam information about locals. Even the children ran to the other side of the street if they saw him approaching for fear that he would vent his anger on them.

And one afternoon after school, Sarah found a girl from fifth class trembling in the yard, too terrified to walk home alone because Geraghty had beaten her earlier that day for looking in the window of his shop. It made Sarah more careful than ever when alone in the cottage.

On the following Wednesday, two letters arrived.

The first had a Dublin postmark and was handwritten by Michael Collins.

He expressed his sadness that they had still not discovered any information about Sean. However, he wanted to reassure her that they would not give up until they brought him home. She found the letter comforting as some days she worried that with all the mayhem in the country, Sean had been forgotten even by his own men.

The second letter came from Maddie who was now back in London. Although dismayed by news of Sean's disappearance she urged Sarah to be optimistic about his safe return. And she could not contain her excitement and delight at the news of Sarah's pregnancy, which spilled over into several pages. Finally, she revealed that she had already bought little outfits for the baby in neutral shades which she would give to Sarah when she travelled to London.

Maddie's letter instilled hope as it reminded her that things were now at their lowest ebb and could only get better and she longed to see Maddie face to face. She even decided to take the train to Dublin on the following Saturday and go to Clerys department store where she would find all she required to knit a few matinee coats for her baby. The thought filled her with excitement as she fried bacon, eggs, and black pudding.

In recent days, the morning sickness had gone completely but her appetite had doubled, and she was concerned about putting on a lot of weight. It was one thing concealing her burgeoning belly with a corset and bandaging but it would be more difficult to account for a sudden increase in weight, especially when men and women alike had always commented on her slim, elegant figure. The more she thought about it the more she realised that she would have to review her attire, with flowing lines and colourful scarves to divert attention away from her ever-expanding stomach and she rued the day she had lied about her marital status.

A tiny voice from within berated her.

Why did I not explain my husband's absence by saying that he was working in England or even America?

She knew that if she told the truth now about her marital status, they would run her out of the village as a liar and a fallen woman, whose word counted for nothing. There was no other option but to leave for England once the summer holidays arrived. In the meantime, she had to be extra careful because she was determined to get every wage packet that she could until then. On Saturday, she would look for dress patterns in Clery's store which could be altered by adding extra details to the collar and cuffs, so drawing the eye away from the waistline.

Chapter Fifteen

On Friday, the sound of yellowhammers singing in a heavenly chorus in the tall poplar trees at the end of the garden drifted in through her slightly open window. She liked to think that they were paying homage to the glory of the world and the long summer ahead. Jumping out of bed she pushed up the sash window and allowed rays of sunlight to flood the room. Late primroses and cowslips were still visible in her back garden while bluebells spread a purple-blue carpet under the trees and along the grassy banks.

Then she heard a haunting, primitive sound that made her look up into the sky, it was the distinctive call of wild geese as they communicated with each other.

A large skein was flying directly overhead in a v-shaped formation having wintered locally in Glenbeg bog. She leaned out and craned her neck as they continued in a north-westerly direction on their way to summer feeding grounds near the North pole. She had heard old people say that they were portents of change or even death. When they disappeared, she dressed hurriedly and made her way to the kitchen where embers still glowed in the range from the night before. While waiting for the kettle to sing, she stood at the open door and worked out a plan for the morning class. Her pupils were now so giddy with the onset of warm weather and longer hours of daylight that their attention spans were dwindling by the hour. She decided to divide the morning between arithmetic and spellings in Irish and English. Afterwards, she would teach them about plants and astronomy. Although not on the curriculum she tried to spend at least one afternoon per month telling them stories about the planets. Their favourite concerned *Cassiopeia's Chair* named after the vain Queen of Ethiopia in Greek mythology. And they would sit with rapt attention as the tale unfurled about her vanity which caused her to be bound to a chair and set in the heavens for all time, revolving around the north celestial pole in an upside-down position.

Once, just as Sarah was delivering the last line of her story amidst a chorus of whistles and clapping from her senior pupils, Fr. Daly had arrived out of the blue and stormed into the classroom demanding to know why the children were behaving raucously.

While Sarah explained that she was trying to impart general knowledge to them about the wider world he banged his walking stick several times on the bare wooden floor to vent his fury. Then to the amazement of her pupils, he rebuked Sarah.

"This is a Catholic school, who gave you permission to waste time on pagan superstitions?"

Her reply was acerbic.

"I was merely trying to give them some knowledge of Greek and Roman myths. Do you not believe that we owe a lot to ancient civilizations? For example, Plato and Aristotle."

His face had turned purple like a beetroot.

"I believe Miss Murphy that you have lost the run of yourself! You are not teaching upper-class pupils in Eton or Harrow! The three Rs are what matters here:

Reading, Writing and Arithmetic."

Sarah was about to protest at his narrow thinking, but he hurried from the room, muttering to himself:

"The teacher in the upside-down chair."

Later, Sarah discovered gossip had spread throughout the village about the priest's anger and how he had given her a moniker. And she often wondered with amusement if that was the nickname her pupils used behind her back.

"It implies that I am heading for the madhouse."

She had confided in Sean who laughed it off with a few astute words.

"Children have always found nicknames for their teachers. Don't worry about it."

Thereafter, she always posted a young watchman outside the school door whenever she broached Greek or Roman mythology.

Suddenly, steam spurted from the spout of the heavy black bottomed kettle and she stopped daydreaming as she hurried back to the range. Then, removing it from the heat she made a small pot of tea which she placed on the table alongside a book entitled; *A Popular History of Astronomy during the Nineteenth Century.*

She could hardly wait to tell her pupils more facts from that famous book written by a Skibbereen woman; Agnes Clerke and given to her by Sean, also a native of Cork.

She opened the book slowly and allowed her fingers to follow the lines of his bold handwriting, in black ink.

To my precious Sarah,

All my Love,

Sean.

He had bought it in London on their honeymoon along with a green silk scarf which he said made her look like a goddess from another planet.

Sighing, she turned the pages of the book quickly as she tried to concentrate on its contents. The trouble was that since Sean's disappearance everything she saw or touched seemed to remind her of him.

Lately, she had cleared the small bedside table in her room and placed some of his old classical sheet music on it, along with a tiny photograph of him as a young boy with his beloved collie dog. It helped her cling to the hope that he would return safely.

Just as she was filling her cup with tea, she felt a strange fluttering like movement in her stomach and guessed that it must be the baby's first kick. For some minutes she placed both hands on her belly but could feel nothing. Yet, it helped her realise how fortunate she was to be expecting Sean's child because no matter what happened she would still always be connected to him. It gave her confidence too to approach the magistrate again about the identity of her real father. She would bet every penny which she possessed that he was not telling the full truth and she was determined to uncover it.

On the following Friday, she was cycling into the village one evening when she spotted his motor car stopped outside Tuohy's public house, which was next door to the courthouse. She paused near the butcher's shop and pretended to fix the chain on her bicycle as he emerged and got into the driver's seat, while his chauffeur took the passenger one.

After what seemed like an interminable amount of time and several attempts to get it started, they eventually moved off at an infuriatingly slow pace leaving small pools of black oil on the street. When they passed her by, she stifled a laugh because she caught a look of elation on his face as he sat bolt upright with his two hands glued to the steering wheel.

"Old fool, three sheets in the wind!"

She muttered to herself as she saw them turn a corner and miss by a whisker, a horse and cart coming in the opposite direction. She decided to follow them home and use the element of surprise to extract more information from him. While he had told her not to ask again about her real father, she reckoned that his guard would be down after several Jameson whiskeys.

When she eventually reached the rusty gates of the old Glebe she dismounted from her bicycle and propped it against them. Then taking a short cut through a cluster of ash trees she arrived at the back of the house where she found the chauffeur tinkering with the engine of the car. He doffed his cap to her, and she responded with a business-like demeanour.

"Good evening, I am here to see His Honour, about an important matter relating to school."

He chuckled and she caught a whiff of alcohol from him.

"Follow me, his old housekeeper Mrs Black has a snooze at this time every evening so I will take you to him myself. He is in the study, he had a few too many, I fear."

She followed in silence through narrow passageways until he paused at a grey door and knocked lightly on it.

"Come!"

Sarah felt giddy with apprehension as she recognised the magistrate's voice.

The chauffeur opened the door gingerly.

"Your Honour, I have a lady here who wishes to speak with you."

The magistrate who was slumped by the fire in a green leather armchair jumped up when he saw Sarah. Rubbing his eyes which were bloodshot he pulled out a chair for her and beckoned to the chauffeur to leave them alone.

She sat down opposite him as he examined her face.

Then he poured more alcohol into a glass on the small, round table nearby.

"Goddam - it! I know your face and those -eyes -those eyes, I have seen them before many years ago -that's it!"

He paused for a moment to give a deep cough.

"You have Molly's eyes - so that makes you my daughter."

"Your -daughter! I don't think so."

Sarah looked at him dubiously.

"Yes. You are my daughter- even though I never admitted it."

The words were slurred and barely audible as he swallowed a mouthful from his glass.

Sarah was astonished but she was determined to get facts from him.

"I am known as Sarah Murphy, but I asked you a few weeks back about my real father. You said he was an officer -." Her voice trailed off.

He nodded but it was obvious that his mind was elsewhere.

She was determined to prise as much information from him as possible.

"You are regarded as a wise, hard-working magistrate so you can understand that I need to know more about my roots. You said my real father was a friend of yours and that he had a dalliance with my mother - your young housekeeper, which resulted in my birth."

He threw his head back and guffawed loudly and she could see that he was heavily intoxicated.

"I - remember now…."

He stood up, swayed for a second and then sat down again.

"Sarah Murphy my eye! You are my daughter - you were born on the wrong side of the blanket - your Mother was our housekeeper but I was already married - she was a beauty just like you -and I fell for her charms."

He paused and took another sip while she suppressed the shock welling up inside her because she wanted to hear more.

"Do please continue, Your Honour," she said coaxingly.

"Well, I - was in deep trouble at the time if word got out to my superior or my wife so I concocted a story about a friend of mine - having his - wicked way with your mother."

He chuckled to himself as he rocked over and back.

Sarah felt the blood rush to her head at his cavalier attitude, but she bit her lip hard until she could taste blood. She had to stop herself from saying anything which might make him clam up.

In a low voice she said, "So, you fathered the child - not some dead army man?"

He nodded.

"That's the truth, the whole truth and nothing but the truth – this is like one of my -courts."

He laughed raucously at his own attempt at humour.

Sarah protested.

"I don't know what to believe. One day you say my father is some high and mighty friend of yours. Now you state that you are my real father."

"I can prove it! Otherwise, why would I pay for your upkeep - until you reached the age of 16years?"

He staggered across the room and rummaged through the top drawer of a walnut bureau.

"Blast it! I cannot find it now. "

She studied him from underneath her lashes.

After a few minutes, he took a swipe at a stack of papers resting on top of the bureau. And they flew across the floor in every direction.

She was about to pick them up when he shouted.

"Leave them!"

Muttering to himself he returned to his chair.

"I was looking for the key to the press in the library. I wanted to show you proof that I paid money twice a year into an account in Woodcocks Bank in Sackville Street."

Sarah was stunned and played with the button on her jacket.

He slurred his words as he pointed a finger in her direction.

"How did you think your grandmother managed to provide for you?"

She gave him a piercing look.

"She was a seamstress and made everything from communion frocks to habits for the deceased, she taught my mother to sew too. And my great uncle Daniel in America sent her dollars for my birthday and Christmas and towards my education."

He sniggered

"That's what she told you. Did you ever see a letter from that uncle or a stack of dollars arriving in the post?"

She wanted to slap him across the face and bring him to his senses.

Instead, she conceded.

"No. He always sent it through the bank so that it would not be stolen. But I do recall Granny going to Woodcock's bank every December and April. Granny explained that he could read but not write and he did not want his wife to know that he was sending money to support me because they had a family of their own."

He gave a slap to the table.

"Think about it my dear – you can see why she made up that story about some relative – it was to protect you from hearing the truth about me and causing a second scandal as you grew up."

Sarah thought for a moment.

"She had to admit that despite his drunken state he seemed to be telling the truth."

He leaned forward.

"She had already helped avert – one scandal - by encouraging Molly to go along with my arrangement."

Sarah pondered his words for a few minutes.

Then with her face a blazing red she remarked.

"So, Granny knew all along that the marriage to that creep Murphy was just a cover-up."

He nodded his head as his eyes grew drowsy

"If only you were my legit - imate daughter ... when I kick the bucket everything will go to my nephew in Dub ..."

He failed to finish his sentence because his eyes closed, and his head fell back against the high back of the chair.

For several minutes Sarah sat immobilised with shock.

When she was satisfied that he was in a deep sleep she stood up and scrutinised him, but the drunken features and loud boar-like snoring repulsed her. She ran from the room with tears flooding down her face.

Later, when she tried to recall escaping the stultifying atmosphere of that old house, she had neither memory of leaving it nor of the journey home on her bicycle.

It was all a blank when she awoke with a start to find herself lying on her bed, still fully dressed at 6 am the next morning. All she could think about was William Taylor's revelation that he was her real father, and it spun around and around inside her head while she washed and changed into fresh clothes. She wished that she was able to dismiss it as just the ramblings of a drunken man, but she sensed that he was speaking the truth. Despite his slurring of certain words, he had spoken with authority, not like someone who was just making it up. And everything he said, seemed to fit in a strange way with fragments of information which she knew including details about the bank.

She had often heard Rita remark about drunken talk often reflecting the real story.

And now she was convinced that for the first time he had spoken the truth to her.

For the next two weeks, thoughts about Taylor occupied every moment of her time when she was not busy teaching. She still had so many unanswered questions relating to him and his relationship with her mother. And she wrote a long letter to Maddie in which she hinted that she had reason to believe the local magistrate was her father. However, she was careful to send a much more casual one to Rita, as she felt that her aunt had enough to cope with in Belfast without adding to her worries, with revelations about William Taylor.

May Day or Lá Bealtaine as she insisted the children call it, fell on a Thursday that year and brought warm, sunny weather. Traditionally, it marked the first day of summer and a busy time on the local estates owned by the gentry as well as on the small, subsistence holdings. For Sarah, it meant that the children were too excited to sit at their desks.

Instead, she took them for a nature walk through the warren of pathways in the bog and along narrow lanes where wildflowers abounded. They gathered armfuls of marigolds, primroses, and buttercups which they carried back to the school. There they made a little altar with a statue to the Virgin Mary surrounded with jam jars which they filled with their flowers and water from the nearby holy well.

Afterwards, they drew lots to decide who should decorate the hawthorn bush at the front of the school with ribbons because it was believed that such practises brought good luck for the year.

When school was over, she went straight home and spent the remainder of the afternoon seated in her favourite armchair, knitting a bonnet for the baby. To the clackety-clack of the needles, her mind went over all she had ever heard about William Taylor, her putative father. She must have dozed off because she was awakened much later by a persistent knocking on the front door. The wall clock showed twenty minutes to eight as she glanced out the window and recognised the overweight figure and mottled skin of a neighbour known as Babbie Newman.

When she drew back the locks on the door the woman's lips curled into a slight sneer.

"It's like Kilmainham Gaol here with all the locks and bolts! I have brought you a pound of butter and fresh milk straight from my two fine cows. Here take them."

Sarah smiled politely as she accepted the slab of butter wrapped in old brown paper and the big jug of milk with blue stripes on it.

"Thank you, Babbie. Please come inside for a cup of tea, I have some currant bread which will go well with your butter."

Babbie moved her head from side to side.

"No thanks, Miss Murphy I am in a hurry as I want to give the toddler a bath before her bedtime, she was outside all day making mud pies with the older ones. I hope you don't think I am rude, if I had more time I would love to sit and talk."

Sarah's eyes twinkled.

"Not at all, don't you worry. Even though I am a Dubliner, I know about this custom. If you don't give butter and milk to your neighbour on May Day, your cows won't produce milk for the rest of the year."

"Holy God! You have learned a lot about country living!"

"Yes, the boys and girls tell me all about the old ways!" Sarah said.

"That reminds me, I want to thank you for being so patient with young Patricia."

"It's my job." Sarah smiled.

"The master used to beat her because she was slow at sums and reading. Now, she is like a different girl, she can read all the letters that arrive from my sister in America."

"That's great news, Babbie. She is an endearing child and you should be proud of her. Will you wait while I empty this milk into one of my own bowls so that you can take the jug home with you?"

"Don't worry Miss Murphy, I can collect it another day. Good evening to you."

"Good evening to you too Babbie and thanks again."

Sarah watched her until she reached the garden gate and turned right in the direction of her home. Then she closed and secured the bolts on the door and headed for the tiny pantry at the back of the kitchen where she placed the butter and milk. She was just filling the kettle with water from a pail when she heard a few gentle raps on the front door. She assumed that it was Babbie who had changed her mind and decided to collect her jug after all. So, she poured the creamy milk into a white enamel bowl and rinsed out the blue and white vessel before she hurried towards the door.

Pulling back the bolts quickly she opened it to reveal the menacing form of Mel Geraghty outlined in the doorway. He had a huge armful of cuckooflowers interspersed with cow parsley and May blossom.

"I brought these for you as they will cleanse you of your powers! Only a witch like you could make my son disappear!"

His features were contorted with hate.

"I am no witch! Stop talking nonsense!" Sarah exclaimed.

He retorted.

"It's all true. I just worked out that you took Eamonn to the 'Hill of the Witch' near Oldcastle, and that is the reason why he has not been seen since."

Realising that he believed every word that he was spouting it seemed to her that evil personified was standing at her door. She gasped in horror as he pushed her aside with lightning speed and made his way into the tiny sitting room.

She followed him, while her breath came in short gasps.

The room was shadowy, illuminated by ghostly fingers of twilight.

He stood at the fireplace, hands thrust in his pockets, the flowers and foliage strewn at his feet.

Pausing in the narrow doorway and backlight by the flickering of an oil lamp in the hall, she seemed like a spectre to him.

"You have all the hallmarks of a witch! Living here like an old dried-up spinster! Where is he?"

He pointed a thick stubby finger in her direction.

"I told you several times that I have no idea where Eamonn is. Now, please leave."

She spoke very slowly and correctly, determined not to reveal the fear gripping her body but she felt his eyes on her and she heard his heavy breathing.

Slowly ever so slowly she began to light the oil lamp on the table, but he took a few steps and stood behind her with his hand hovering over her head.

Startled, she dropped it as splinters from the glass dome flew in every direction.

"You are a clumsy hag! I will show you what a man does to a woman," he roared.

She turned in the direction of the door, but he grabbed her by the shoulder and swung her around like a rag doll. A nauseating smell of stale porter erupted from his mouth as his reptilian-like tongue shot between her lips. Clenching her jaws, she bit hard on it and he let out a string of curses as she escaped his clutches.

"So, you like the thrill of the chase, do you?"

He said as his left hand dropped and fumbled at the lower buttons on his trousers.

With her lungs resembling a bellows, she rushed to the fireplace and grabbed the big brass poker.

Then, taking one wide swing she delivered a blow to the side of his skull which brought him to his knees, and he screamed in pain.

Before he had a chance to get back on his feet, she hit him again and again until he keeled over.

Horrified, she watched as bright red blood gushed from a gaping wound in his head and a deep gurgling sound escaped from his mouth.

Then the poker fell from her hands as fear paralysed her and silence reigned in that house.

For a long time, she was afraid to make the slightest sound, convinced that he would regain his strength and attack again. Only the ticking of the clock on the wall reminded her that this was real and not some terrifying nightmare.

Eventually, in the eerie moonlight which splayed across his body, she crept from the room and returned with the lamp from the hallway.

Slowly, she made her way through the splinters of glass and crushed flowers to where he lay with his mouth gaping wide and his eyes open.

Steeling herself she felt for a pulse but could find none.

From head to toe, her body was shaking at the enormity of what she had done but she shuffled to her bedroom and returned with a hand mirror. Placing it across his mouth several times it remained clear without the slightest trace of any fogging on it. Touching his hands, she found that they were already cool.

It left her in no doubt about the fact that she had killed him, right there in her own space where she had carved out a fragile peace despite the maelstrom all around her. Yet, he had shattered that peace with his rapacious ways. And she told herself that he had deserved to pay the ultimate price; death.

Quickly, she pulled a tablecloth from a drawer and flung it over his lifeless body.

Then as if frozen to the spot she stood and watched, while a voracious red stain seemed to gobble up the pure white linen.

Chapter Sixteen

Her mouth was bone dry and her clothes were saturated with sweat.

She needed a drink but the thought of re-entering the house filled her with dread.

For several minutes she had paced back and forth across the soft mossy grass in the back garden.

Oblivious to the celestial beauty of the night sky, she whispered over and over as if to an unseen watcher in the darkness.

"I killed a man -I killed a man - I killed a man -."

Suddenly, her head swung from right to left and she stopped dead in her tracks.

Fear was coursing through her veins.

Was that a human scream drowning out the other sounds of the night?

Had she been mistaken about Geraghty

Was he still alive?

Another screech followed by a longer one filled the air.

Taking several deep breaths, it occurred to her that they were the deep sounds of nocturnal birds of prey communicating with each other across the wild open spaces of the bog.

Tonight, she was too distracted to distinguish between the different calls.

The sense of relief was so great that she felt giddy, but the image of the corpse lying in a pool of blood in her cottage assailed her.

She broke into a run. Around and around the garden in a circle.

She had to put coherence in her thoughts.

Hiding the body was not a real option. She would need help to drag it outside and across the fields before dumping it in the bog, but there was no one she could trust.

Her head was pounding. It would be daylight in a few hours.

She reverted to a childhood habit of talking out loud to herself, as her thoughts seemed to come in waves.

"The murder of an informer is a chance for the leaders in Dublin Castle to unearth more information about locals."

For a few minutes, she stopped and leaned against a tree. Then she took off again around the garden.

"I will be tortured until I tell everything even about Sean."

A noise from the bushes made her stop in her tracks as if frozen to the spot.

Then a small hedgehog appeared and scurried off in the direction of a hedge.

After taking several deep breaths, she started to pace the garden path as if addressing a companion.

"Even a fool can see that I will swing at the end of a rope along with my baby."

She placed her hand on her belly.

She had almost forgotten that she was carrying another little human being, who depended totally on her. She must leave immediately before he was reported missing at the local RIC barracks because she would be among the list of suspects and they would head for her cottage.

Drumming her fingers on her forehead like someone who had just escaped from a lunatic asylum, she decided to cycle to Kilmessan. There she would catch the first train to Dublin and lie low in the safe house kept by the Mulroy family until false ID papers were obtained for her. Then a trip on the mail boat from Dublin to Hollyhead, followed by a train journey to London where she would be safe at Maddie's flat in Ealing.

Seconds later, she gripped the handle of the back door and turned it.

Hesitating, she braced herself for what was to come.

Then screwing her eyes shut she stepped inside and listened as she counted to ten.

All was silent.

She crept to her bedroom, pouring water from the jug on the washstand into a basin. Meticulously, she scrubbed her face and then her hands until they bled with carbolic soap.

Checking her blouse and cardigan she found traces of blood on them and to her horror a large red bloodstain on her skirt. These she abandoned in a heap on the floor and washed her body frantically, before putting on fresh clothes.

Heaving a small suitcase from the top of the wardrobe she began to pack.

Other than a blue suit and some underwear she would have to forfeit the rest of her belongings. She wanted to leave space for a few treasured mementoes of Sean.

When the case was full, she snapped it shut, with a sigh of relief.

After a frantic search underneath the floorboards and behind the chimney of the fireplace in the spare bedroom, she located some personal papers along with jewellery and the locket with Sean's photograph. The papers soon went up in smoke in a small fire which she lit in the grate, while the jewellery was hidden in a stocking pinned to her corset.

Glancing in the dressing table mirror she caught sight of her own reflection. Her bun had come undone and her hair hung limply around her face, like a woman she had seen the previous week queuing outside the workhouse. Grabbing several hairpins, she piled her hair on top of her head and secured it in a tight twist.

She had one last thing to do before escaping. Her savings were hidden in an old Jacobs biscuit tin under the sewing machine in the room where the corpse lay.

She released the door slowly and peered through the narrow opening.

Then, with her heart beating furiously, she pushed it back until she had a view of the entire room.

The pungent smell of blood came rushing out and made her convulse.

She withdrew and took deep breaths.

The sign of the cross, which she made several times gave her strength.

Then, she dug her nails into her wrists and faced back into a scene from hell.

He lay sideways, his face and torso still covered by the tablecloth which had turned a hideous shade of purple. While his lower body and legs protruded grotesquely in a pool of stinking blood. She sidled by the corpse, covering her nose and mouth as a metallic odour emanated from it. Flinging open the window she swallowed large mouthfuls of the fresh night air.

When she noticed that the buckle of his belt was undone, a scream rose from deep in her stomach and pierced the silence of the cottage.

It was a macabre reminder of the reason why she had snuffed out his life like a candle.

A man so consumed by hate for her that he intended to rape her.

Grabbing the biscuit tin, she edged past him and ran from the room. It was only in the hallway that she allowed the tears, pressing at the corners of her eyes, to be released. They raced down her cheeks as if a dam had burst.

It was almost sunrise.

Sweat was pouring down her body.

She stuffed a pile of pound notes and ten shilling notes between the pages of arithmetic books and hid them at the bottom of her brown satchel, which she used for school. Then, handling her Webley revolver with care, she wrapped it in silk lingerie and placed it in the bag too.

Finally, she got large jars of Ponds face cream, marked with the labels "Day Cream", "Night Cream" and put them in on top. She reasoned that if an official at Dun Laoghaire Port enquired about the contents of her satchel, she could say it was filled with cosmetics and books.

She did one last thing before leaving the cottage. A bottle of Yardley's Lily of the Valley cologne stood forlornly on her dressing table. Seizing it, she dabbed it liberally all over her neck, temples, wrists and at her ankles. The sweet, heady scent of the flower essence made her cough, but it was preferable to the lingering odour of blood that seemed to cling to her clothes and every pore of her body.

Darkness was bowing to the light, with streaks of copper and gold radiating from the sun, as she prepared her bicycle. The incongruity of such ethereal beauty after the nightmarish scene which she had just left filled her with awe.

Studying her surroundings, she took strength from the new light which enveloped the landscape. And when the first thrushes bravely warbled in the apple trees followed by a heavenly chorus from wrens and blackbirds, she took it as a sign that everything would be all right once she left that god-forsaken place.

It seemed to her that she was still in slow motion.

Pulled back by some force of evil which remained around that fetid corpse.

After, several attempts she fitted the suitcase on the back carrier of her bike and secured it with two pieces of string. The satchel was easier to manage, the strap rested diagonally across her body and the bag rested on her opposite hip, leaving her free to peddle without worries about it catching in the spokes of the wheels.

She went quickly through the garden gate and took one last look at the cottage with its small windows which shone eerily in the pearly light.

For a split second, she thought she saw a figure looking out at her, but after a second glance, she reckoned it was just a shadow because she could not remember extinguishing all the oil lamps.

Shivering, she hopped onto her bicycle and turned left a few yards up the road. Then she sped down the hill at break-neck speed until she reached the old winding lane which would cut a couple of miles off her journey.

Twenty minutes later, Sarah neared the end of that lane. It was still early with not a soul in sight but in the distance, the deep sound of the bells from St. Felim's Abbey rang out.

She needed a rest before turning onto the main road.

She stopped at an old wooden gate leading to a field where workhorses were grazing.

Soon local farmers would be driving animals to the fair in Dushaughlin. She could not risk drawing attention to herself by fainting due to hunger or exhaustion.

She had no memory of when she had last eaten.

Fortunately, she had some dry biscuits in her coat pocket which she carried around since the morning sickness phase. She ate them quickly, washing them down with some ice-cold water from a nearby stream, cupping her hands to trap the liquid like a child.

Then she was distracted by a commotion from the road.

It was coming closer.

She could hear the grinding thud of an engine.

It was some sort of motorised vehicle.

She crouched in the ditch but made a peephole through some branches. It gave her a clear view of the gap where the lane petered out onto the main road.

It seemed like her ribcage might explode with fear while her mind sought answers to a string of questions.

Can it possibly be a search party out looking for Mel Geraghty?

Have they already discovered his battered body in my cottage?

Did someone see him coming to my cottage with his armful of weeds?

Shrill noises and ear-splitting shouts made her strain her neck.

One Crossley tender full of Black and Tans flashed by followed a few minutes later by a second one, again with Black and Tans.

Then all was quiet.

She strained hard to hear if any birds were singing. It seemed to her that the world had stopped and that this unearthly stillness would last forever.

She could not tell for how long she remained in that position, but a voice in her head repeated.

I am like Lot's wife who was turned into a pillar of salt.

Then she became aware of movement.

The smell of tobacco smoke.

A male voice, beside her.

A firm hand on her shoulder.

Grey, rheumy eyes set in a weather-beaten face.

Her head shook visibly as she looked up at him.

"Did you fall off your bike?" He spoke in a sing-song fashion,

"No. I mean yes. Look, I am not sure what happened or how I ended up in this ditch."

Sarah hoped he would believe her lies.

"Here, hold onto my hand. You don't want to scratch your face with May bush. The fairies might not like it!"

He chuckled at his own attempt at humour.

She took his gnarled old hand and leaned on it as she eased herself out of the bushes.

"My name is Damian but everyone around knows me as Damo. Do you need help?"

She stood up straight and blinked at the daylight which for a moment seemed like it might blind her. When her eyes grew accustomed to her surroundings she answered.

"No. Thank you so much for your kindness. I will be fine, a toss from a bike never killed me so far!"

A horse neighed and shook his harness restlessly. She looked around and saw a Connemara pony with a cart full of potatoes stopped further down the lane.

The man removed his plaid cap, scratched his bald head and then put it back on.

"I could not just leave you lying in the ditch like that! So, I decided to stop and make sure you were alive."

"Thank you for your concern. Earlier, I saw Black and Tans speeding by on the main road. Can you tell me if something happened around here last night?"

He grinned to reveal toothless gums.

"Aye. The big bridge just outside Blackhill village was blown up last night! It looks like it was a bunch of local IRA lads!"

She swallowed.

"But that's the only road from this side which goes all the way to Kilmessan train station. It will cause havoc."

"It will show those British bastards above in Dublin that they don't rule the countryside."

He wiped his nose on his sleeve.

"Indeed, it will show them."

She said in a low voice, but her mind was swirling at this latest development.

"Now, let me check your bicycle before I go. We don't want you stuck here all day with a puncture."

She feigned a smile of gratitude as he lifted the bike out of the ditch and examined it for a few minutes. Then satisfied that it was in working order he patted the suitcase, which was still strapped to the carrier.

"Going anywhere special?" He enquired.

"No. I am just on my way to spend a few days with an old friend."

"You take care, miss!"

He smiled broadly at her and then headed in the direction of the waiting beast.

"Thanks for your help." She called, as he glanced back in her direction and lifted his cap in recognition of her appreciation.

She waited and waited until she was satisfied that he was out of sight.

Her suitcase had to go. It would only arouse suspicion especially with the Black and Tans combing the area for suspects.

It was almost impossible to release the tight knots which held the string around the suitcase.

Her fingers ached and she cursed at the sight of her own blood as the coarse fibres cut her fingers.

There was only one solution.

Without a knife, she would have to bite it with her teeth.

Trembling, she bent down and gnawed on the twine.

Eventually, she succeeded, and the suitcase fell to the ground. She heaved it across the lane and flung it into a deep dyke.

Wheeling her bike, she ventured onto the main road.

There was not a soul to be seen anywhere. Apart from a blackbird feeding its young in a tree hollow. It reminded her of a scene from the Apocalypse.

A couple of hundred yards down the road, enormous black clouds of smoke were rising from a thatched cottage that was on fire.

A rough female voice nearby startled her.

"Get out of here! Before some harm befalls you!"

She looked around and saw a bedraggled woman climbing over a rusty fence. She carried a bucket of milk straight from a red and white cow which was nibbling at patchy grass in a nearby field.

She stopped and pointed a tobacco-stained finger in Sarah's face.

"Are you mad? The Tans set Donnellan's place ablaze! And they will be back. Mark my words."

Sarah's fingers gripped the handlebars of her bike tightly.

The woman gave a raspy cough.

"The wind is blowing the smoke this way. It's hard to breathe."

Sarah wiped her eyes which were stinging from the noxious smoke billowing in their direction.

"Tell me, why did the Tans pick on the Donnellan family?" She asked.

The woman's face turned red with exasperation.

"The Tans think that Andy Donnellan the eldest son was involved in the trouble last night over in Blackhill. But when they called there this morning only his mother made an appearance, so they ransacked the cottage and outhouses before they set it all on fire."

"They are worse than vermin, but where is Mrs Donnellan now?"

"They beat her across the shoulders with the butt of a rifle, because she refused to talk. Mrs Finn her neighbour is looking after her."

Sarah managed a polite nod of the head.

"Miss, what brings you to these parts?"

Sarah looked the woman in the eyes.

"I intended to get the early train to Dublin but with the bridge blown up, I could not reach the railway station. I have a sick aunt in Munster Street who needs my help with a houseful of children."

The woman screwed up her face.

"You could still make it to the city by nightfall if you do as I say."

"Tell me, please." Sarah urged.

"Firstly, you may abandon that bike! There is a right of way through the Kilboyne estate and after that, I am going to send you across a few miles of fields and bog."

Sarah nodded. "That's fine, you can keep my bicycle or sell it if you wish."

The woman's eyes opened wide with delight.

"I will give it to my daughter, she is a parlour maid in the big house near Bective. On her day off she will be able to cycle home for a visit."

"Good," Sarah said tapping her foot impatiently on the ground. "Please give me directions, as you said those 'Tans' might return at any minute."

The woman bent down and drew a map on the dusty ground as she explained the proposed route.

Sarah took out a pencil from her satchel and scribbled the directions hurriedly on the back of a cigarette packet while the woman began to repeat them.

"Hold it there!" Sarah interjected. "Did I hear you say that I would pass by the back of the magistrate's residence?"

"That's right. It's an old Glebe house. He did not take too kindly to the house they gave him when he first arrived in Meath. He thought it was haunted so he ran out of it!"

Sarah could feel her face burning at the mention of her putative father.

The woman continued.

"Use it as a landmark. When you have travelled six or seven miles across country through bogland and woodland you will think that you are lost. So, watch out for the tall chimneys of the Glebe which you will see a long way off."

"Are you are sending me in a circle?" Sarah asked with incredulity.

"Yes, once you reach the Glebe you are just 6 or 7 miles from the main road into Ashbourne. It will be easy to get a lift on a horse and cart, many of them will be going into the city."

Sarah cleared her throat, she did not like the sound of waiting around on the main road into the city, where she could be apprehended for murder.

But another plan was forming in her head.

Her main priority was to get as far away as possible from the scene of the crime while at the same time avoiding any chance encounters with the Black and Tans.

"Thank you, you have been a great help." Sarah gave her a weak smile.

The woman nodded but her eyes had already moved to Sarah's bike glinting in the early morning sunshine.

Sarah set off on foot with her satchel still across her body, along a right of way used by wayfarers, vagabonds, and rovers since ancient times.

Chapter Seventeen

On that early summer morning, the magnificent beauty of the countryside filled her with great sadness. A patchwork of fields filled with lines of flowery potato ridges and corn ripening in the sun spread out before her. She wished that it could be just a normal day and that she was out with her pupils for a walk, teaching them to respect all God's creatures, instead of running like an escaped convict through the countryside.

Then a voice in her head ridiculed her.

You didn't respect Mel Geraghty – you murderer.

She tried to quell it by humming baby lullabies, but the voice became more persistent.

You knew from that night at the Ceili in 1913 that getting involved with Sean would lead you *into trouble – and now you are on the road to perdition.*

Unable to bear it any longer she started to recite poems in Irish at the top of her voice which she had learned from Sean, who was a fluent Irish speaker.

At length, she took a break and sat in the shade under a horse chestnut tree where she ate the last of her dry biscuits. The branches adorned with candle-like flowers had cuckoo spit on them. She remembered as a child believing that it was spit left by cuckoos. Later she had discovered it had nothing at all to do with cuckoos but was made by a sap-sucking insect.

There was a small stream nearby and she swallowed the cool clear water in gulps until she had satiated her thirst.

Then, lying back on the soft grass she closed her eyes and rested. She thought of all the nights Sean had slept under the stars on his way to and from a safe house. And she recalled the wonderful days she had spent with him camping in Wicklow.

Somewhere in her mind, a voice whispered.

Is he imprisoned in some dark makeshift prison now?

She silenced her own black thoughts by talking gently to her baby in the womb.

My darling baby, I have so much to tell you about the world and its ways.

Eventually, she dozed off and dreamt that she was on a merry-go-round with all the children from her school.

When she awoke, she heard church bells in the distance.

Checking her watch, it pointed at six o'clock.

Totally exhausted, she had slept for several hours, despite the hard ground.

Still groggy, she forced herself to move on.

She had to find somewhere safe to spend the night.

If all went well, she would hide in one of the disused stables at the Glebe.

It was a daring plan.

However, she reasoned that the last place the constabulary would look for a murderer would be in the magistrate's home. And she was coming very close to the Glebe judging by the woman's directions.

Apart from a few farmers in the distance tending to their crops and a beggar lying in his own vomit she had encountered no one. At night these tracks would be a dangerous place with drunks and scoundrels.

Suddenly, in the distance through the treetops, she saw the top of a chimney.

She hurried on, breathing heavily.

One, two, three, four, five …six. There they were towering proudly into the sky.

She was within minutes of the Glebe.

Tears of relief slid down her face. Her heels were blistered, and her body covered in sweat. And for the last mile, the baby in her belly had kicked as if to will her onwards.

The magistrate's labrador rushed down the stone steps and approached her.

She was hiding behind a giant oak tree, waiting for her chance to slip into one of the old stables. There was no sign of the motor car or the chauffeur, but the back door was wide open.

The dog approached her gingerly. Then he sniffed at her shoes and her legs for a few seconds. With her heart in her mouth, she prayed silently that he would not bark.

She extended her fingers and he licked them as his tail wagged furiously.

Stroking him, she spoke in a soft voice.

"Clever boy! You know that we have met before."

After a few minutes, she heard a shrill whistle and he rushed back in the direction of the old glasshouse at the side of the house.

It was at least an hour later when she saw the magistrate emerge with a watering can.

He made his way into the house, slowly. It was the first time she had seen him in stained, casual clothes. He looked like any other older man, tired and arthritic.

It all seemed unreal to her. This stranger, whose name had filled her with hate for so many years was now claiming to be her real father.

She waited until the lamps were light in the house and the curtains closed. Then under the cover of darkness, she slipped into the last stable, the one farthest from the house.

Hunger nagged at her.

She found some apples stored between layers of newspapers in boxes, leftover from the previous autumn. She ate two of them greedily and lay her head down on her satchel as if it were a pillow.

She would leave at dawn.

Then she hoped to slip across the main road and make her way through more fields and byways to the Ward camp outside Ashbourne where she knew Biddy-Anne and her family spent every summer.

Tinkers were loyal to anyone who had shown them kindness.

She would seek their assistance and request that they give her a lift in their horse-drawn wagon into the city.

Fatigue overcame her and she fell asleep.

Hours later, scratching at the door.

Was she having a dream?

More scratching.

A voice.

Sarah rubbed her eyes and sat bolt upright.

Then it all came back to her, she was hiding in a disused stable full of spiders and mice.

More shouts from outside.

She listened.

A creaking noise like a rusty gate.

Daylight flooded in along with a fresh breeze.

A great shadow coming towards her.

The whiff of a dog.

Excited barking.

Followed by great licks on her face from a wet tongue.

She scrambled to her feet and stared straight into the magistrate's face.

He was unshaven and wore a black dressing gown edged with purple.

"Miss Murphy! Why are you sleeping in my stable?"

"I am sorry, Your Honour."

She struggled to offer an explanation.

"I was in the middle of my ablutions when I noticed this clever canine scratching frantically at the stable door.

I have a bird's eye view from my bedroom, I can see the whole back yard."

"I will leave immediately."

She grabbed her satchel from the floor.

"What made you come here last night?" His voice was firm.

She took a few steps in the direction of the door. It was wide open.

"I am waiting, Miss Murphy, for an answer."

The tone had hardened.

Her mind was firing questions at her.

Is this a trap? Has news of Gallagher's callous murder in my cottage *reached him yet?*

"I - I got lost. I set out early yesterday to take the train from Kilmessan station to Dublin, my cousin is sick. The bridge was blown up, so I had to turn back, and I decided to take the old cross-country route this way and go to the city via Ashbourne."

He shook his head, but his features had softened.

"Stupid business! Cutting off a main bridge like that! You cannot carry on in that state …. You must come in-doors and wash."

"Thank you, sir, but I need to keep going. I promised to mind my cousin's children."

"Nonsense! You need to tidy yourself. I insist."

She could not refuse his invitation.

"Thank you, you are very kind."

Her brain was trying to work out the best course of action.

Will I make a run for it?

Or will I go along with him?

"It's Sunday and Mrs Black takes the day off. I am sure she has left some food ready. Once you have made yourself presentable you must join me for breakfast."

"Certainly, Your Honour."

She said, inwardly cursing herself for not leaving at dawn as she had planned.

When she had finished washing in the cavernous bathroom at the top of the stairs, she made her way cautiously back through a warren of passages to the kitchen.

A sly inner voice reminded her.

You could escape now.

Just go!

The satchel bag was slung across her shoulder. It gave her comfort to know that the gun was still resting in it.

The grandfather clock in the hallway chimed slowly.

Her stomach was in knots from tension.

She had to stay and be polite, but the sensible thing was to leave while she still had time.

She was now convinced that news had not yet reached him about the murder.

She had to believe that Geraghty's family just regarded him as a missing person.

She hoped that they would not start to put two and two together until she failed to turn up for school on Monday morning.

The magistrate was preparing a large tray piled high with brown bread, cold hard-boiled eggs, and a silver pot of tea.

"Follow me. One has to be versatile!"

He exclaimed as he carried it proudly into the library, where he placed it on a small table.

She sat opposite him as he directed. And she watched with bated breath while he poured tea into a blue and gold-edged china cup.

Her brain was working overtime.

You abandoned my mother?

You told me lies.

And only in a drunken state revealed that you are my real father.

I could kill you now!

You are nothing but a coward hiding behind the mask of officialdom.

"Miss Murphy, can you hear me?"

She leaned back in her chair and declared.

"It is so strange to be sitting across the table from my real father."

For a split second his right hand hung in the air. Then he counted out lumps of sugar one by one with tiny silver tongs and dropped them into his cup of tea - when he reached four a scarlet colour had spread across his face.

She fixed her gaze on him until he looked her straight in the eyes.

He spoke with false gusto.

"I must say you are not lacking in courage and I applaud you for that."

"I could remind you that at our last meeting you disclosed the true identity of my father."

Her tone was flint-like.

"There is no need to remind me. I know what I told you and I stand by it."

For a few minutes, there was total silence.

She had expected him to deny everything.

He gave her a wry smile.

Suddenly, it seemed to her that all that had passed in the last few days was a necessary course of events. Otherwise, she would not be sitting there, face to face with the local Resident Magistrate, who had finally conceded that he was her father.

She poured milk into the cup of tea beside her and drank it all down in two mouthfuls.

He insisted on refilling her cup and urged her to eat from the food on the table.

She nibbled at some bread and a hard-boiled egg while he spoke.

"Miss Murphy, I am an old man, I won't live forever."

She raised her eyebrows.

"What do you mean, Your Honour?"

He coughed.

"It is thanks to several pills that I get through the days. Now, the nights are a different matter … I sleep for two at the most three hours. Then, they all come calling… they seem to advance on me in waves. my deceased son and his family … screaming for help … they went down with Titanic…"

She gave him a knowing nod of her head but refrained from speaking lest she stop him from going on.

He rose from his chair and pointed at the decanter of brandy on the sideboard.

"Without that elixir, I could not carry on. It is my only real friend."

Then he dropped back into his seat and she sighed inwardly.

He took a sip of tea followed by a long silence.

Finally, a sardonic smile appeared at the edge of his lips.

"During these nightmares, my dearly departed wife visits me … along with your mother."

"My mother?" Sarah enquired unapologetically.

He sat back in his chair.

"They scream at me too but not for help … they both admonish me for betraying them … it is like hell… I cannot keep running… this is my second residence since I moved to Meath."

A new emotion shot through her while she studied this man sitting opposite her.

She bit her lip as she realised that her feelings of hate had been replaced by pity, pity for a narcissistic, pathetic old man.

His expression showed relief.

"Now, you know it all, you may understand why I lied to you."

She shut down the voice of anger which was surging through her again at his latest comment.

He wants my forgiveness, now that he is old-.

Instead, she enquired dispassionately.

"Have you sought help with this?"

He looked bewildered.

"I told you that I take pills, lots of them."

Her voice was measured.

"Have you heard of psychoanalysis? A man called Sigmund Freud is pioneering this method … I believe the aim is to release repressed emotions and experiences. My friend in London has told me all about it."

He studied her closely.

"You know that I am so proud of you … so clever and so well informed. You remind me of a line from Oliver Goldsmith's poem about a schoolmaster, the one that wonders 'how one small head could carry all he knew'."

She remained silent, taken aback by his flattery. She was beginning to realise that this man was like a creature from the moon, she had no idea who he really was under his mask of authority.

He gestured to books on the window ledge.

"I am very fond of Oliver Goldsmith's work. You know a distant relative of mine studied in Trinity college with the great man. They got up to all kinds of antics - the stories were passed down through the family."

She nodded sagely.

"He was talented. Now, speaking of family I would like to hear more about my own mother?"

He cleared his throat.

"She was pretty and loved to sing to herself as she did the cooking and cleaning."

A silent tear fell from Sarah's left eye.

"What did she sing?"

His face relaxed into a smile.

"The Last Rose of Summer was one of her favourites - I often stood outside the scullery window and listened while she sang it. Her voice was out of the ordinary -."

Sarah shook her head and looked at him in disbelief.

"I never knew she was a singer."

"She was always happy and looked on the bright side until that scoundrel married her - it was all my idea -."

Out of the blue, a shrill prolonged sound like a bell interrupted his flow of speech.

It made her jump.

Then she realised that it was a telephone ringing in the next room.

He dropped his napkin on the table and hurried out to answer it.

A silence so perceptible fell upon that small space that she felt claustrophobic.

She tiptoed to the half-open door, taking in great gulps of air from the hallway.

The pungent smell of beeswax and turpentine from the polished wooden floor assailed her nostrils.

His sonorous voice boomed through the house as he assumed the mask of his rank.

"Yes. Indeed, this is hardly surprising in the circumstances."

A pregnant pause.

"District Inspector, thank you for apprising me of this latest occurrence. Do keep me informed as events unfold -."

An interior monologue unfolded.

They have found the body.

Am I on their wanted list?

Or is this telephone call about other matters?

My head will burst with all these questions.

For a split-second Sarah considered running away, escaping to the open fields.

Silence from the next room while he took in what was being relayed to him.

"Indeed, the rigours of the law must be applied to such persons." He spoke gravely.

Another silence.

Her eyes moved to her satchel bag which lay on a chair.

A chilling voice inside her head nagged again.

If he knows about the murder and wants to detain you until the constabulary arrives - shoot him.

The tinkling sound of the candle phone as he put down the receiver.

She rushed back to her chair and sat primly on the edge of it.

He re-entered the room with his head bowed, lost in thought.

"Your Honour, thank you for your kindness - I must go now."

He walked to the window and gazed outside at the rolling lawn for an interminable amount of time.

The inner voice nagged her.

What will I do?

Leave or repeat the same sentence.

He swung round suddenly and faced her, one knobbly finger held upright.

Her heart sank.

"Do not treat me like a fool, they found the body of Mel Geraghty at your home. I want the whole truth now and I shall then decide on what course of action to take."

"Yes. Your Honour," she said with emphasis on the last word.

His eyes narrowed.

"Drop the obsequious manner I want the plain truth, a daughter talking to her father."

At that moment words flashed across her brain.

There is still hope, he will show the compassion of a father.

Struggling to speak she began tentatively.

"I believe - you know that Mel Geraghty's son left in the middle of the night and never returned."

He moved closer and sat in a green leather armchair.

"Indeed! I heard from my chauffeur that at one stage that odious man suggested I might have had some influence in his son's disappearing act, just because I was civil to the poor boy."

"Well, he shifted all the blame for his son's departure onto me as I used to tutor him outside school. He arrived at my door late on Friday evening - he forced his way into my home and accused me of being a witch who had spirited his son off to some other realm."

"Is that so!"

He said as he concentrated on lighting a fat cigar.

The voice in her head dared her.

Go! Make your escape.

And if he follows you shoot.

He threw a glance at her.

"Go on I am listening."

Sarah spoke slowly and with dignity.

"He was about to violate me - he was full of hate - I just grabbed the poker and I hit him - and then again and again - I had to defend myself - he was like a crazed man."

"Do you mean that he was going to ravish you?"

Tears flowed down her face.

"Yes. He was intent on raping me as he saw me as a witch who needed to be taught a lesson."

His tone softened.

"My dear lady, please stop the tears. I do not need to hear anymore. In fact, the less you implicate me in any of this business the better."

Relief swept over her body. "I should go -."

He offered her a crisp white handkerchief.

She took it and dried her eyes.

"It is fortunate that today is Sunday and I am all alone. You must get as far away from here as possible - I cannot be seen to be hiding a suspected murderer - they believe that he discovered some secret from your past and was black-mailing you."

She looked him in the eye.

"That is untrue."

"I believe you, but he was feeding them with infor-mation on locals and so it makes sense to them. They are hell-bent on extracting information from you about seditious activities in the area and the latest outrage with the bridge. The issue of his murder is not their main priority."

Her heart sank but a voice deep within her cautioned her.

My future now lies in the hands of this man … my puta-tive father.

"I swear that his hatred for me was all about his missing son and that I had nothing to do with the explosion."

He assented.

"Fortunately, I have heard the whispers about him. He hated everyone who was nice to his boy."

Her cheeks still glowed like burning coal, but her heart beat a little less frantically.

"Now, I shall drive you part of the way. I take it that you are not visiting a relative in Dublin but planning an escape from these shores."

She nodded.

"I am much - I mean I cannot say how much this means to me. Thank you. I am indebted to you."

His forehead creased.

"I am only human after all! I could not throw my own daughter to the wolves!"

A tiny voice within her screamed.

Own daughter!

Am I really hearing this from the Resident Magistrate?

His voice was urgent.

"Are you feeling all right?"

"My apologies, I am fine, it's just the lack of sleep," she lied.

In a matter of fact tone he spoke.

"You will need to get a new identity - they are going to circulate your photograph - the port will be watched."

"My photograph! Where did they get one?"

She could not help herself.

"The Catholic priest had one of you taken last year following some event at the school."

She gasped.

"So, he was not slow to hand it over to the law!"

"Don't worry about him, in these extraordinary circumstances we need to hurry. While I am starting up the motor car, go into the basement and you will find old hats belonging to my housekeeper. Pick a big one and hide your hair under it."

She was shaking from head to toe.

"Yes, sir."

He stood up and rummaged through some papers on the mantelpiece.

"Here, take these old spectacles. I got new ones recently. If we are stopped by the Black and Tans, I shall say you are my housekeeper."

She opened her lips, but no words came out.

"Hurry my dear! Time is of the essence."

"I am so grateful to you."

He looked at her wearily.

"I think we both know that my help is long overdue. Besides, I will have to answer to my maker soon."

She exclaimed out loud.

"Please don't say that! Now, that I have just found you!"

He answered in a voice choking with emotion.

"When you are ready wait outside the back door, it will take a few minutes to get the motor car ticking over."

Before she could reply he hurried out of the room with head bent, nervously checking the hands on his pocket watch.

Chapter Eighteen

At half-past ten the black Ford motor car edged its way through the big iron gates.

The magistrate sat poker-straight behind the wheel while he concentrated on the road.

In the back Sarah perched on the edge of the black leather seat with her fingers entwined in the handgrip. The car turned left onto a bog road and proceeded to negotiate pothole after pothole while she tried to avoid being thrown around from one side to another like a rubber ball.

When they reached the tiny village of Kilnish he swung the car up a narrow laneway to avoid the mass goers. They were descending on the church from every direction in various conveyances pulled by donkeys and ponies.

The lane twisted and turned while Sarah held on for her life. Over the noise of the engine, it was impossible to make sense of the magistrate's shouts but she guessed by his gestures that it was a series of expletives about the appalling condition of the lane.

She prayed silently that they would not end up in the ditch. It was clear that he had no patience behind the wheel. Flocks of geese, stray sheep and even an errant horse ran for their lives. By the time they reached a crossroads her hands were bathed in sweat.

He turned right onto a busy road, narrowly missing a butcher's boy, with a sign on his bike which proclaimed; *Meehan's beef, lamb, and pork.*

Then just as they passed the bend in the road, she saw it.

A Crossley Tender full of Black and Tans was blocking the road, while two constabulary officers stood nearby.

Sarah heard the gnashing of brakes as he brought the car to a shuddering halt.

She pulled the hat further down on her head and popped the borrowed spectacles on her nose.

The taller of the officers approached the car.

"Good morning, sir. Can you tell me your name and what is your business in these parts?"

"I am The Honourable William Taylor, Resident Magistrate."

She saw the officer exchange a glance with his colleague before giving a signal to the waiting truck.

He gave a military salute.

"I beg your pardon, Your Honour, there is a lot of nasty stuff going on, first the blowing up of the bridge on Friday night and then the foul murder of a barber. An individual who was most useful to us."

"Indeed. These are troubled times. Now, officer, get that truck out of the way, I am bringing a loyal, old servant to hospital. And be quick!"

"Yes. Your Honour."

Sarah's breathing became more even while the magistrate drummed his fingers on the steering wheel.

The officers ran to perform his bidding. And in less than five minutes the road was cleared.

He put his foot hard to the floor and the car took off with a mighty roar while clouds of smoke enveloped them as they passed by the truck which had moved into a gateway.

When they were out of sight of the Crown's forces he raised his left thumb to indicate that they were free. And then she saw him laughing and talking to himself like a little boy who has just stolen all the cake without the adults noticing anything amiss.

She smiled and leaned forward to return the sign, hoping that he might glance back and see it. However, he was concentrating so hard on the rocky road ahead of him that he was oblivious to her.

On and on they sped, through country roads while hedgerows, fields and cyclists flashed by.

Eventually, they came to a milestone concealed by the verdant vegetation at the side of the road, known as *The Five Mile Stone.*

He stopped the car abruptly and eased himself out painfully. In the strong sunshine, she was startled to see his face which was covered in wrinkles and made him look older than his years. Then he released the passenger door and she emerged.

"My dear lady, I hope this is of some help to you. I dare not go any further. We are just five miles from Dublin Castle - the streets will be crawling with the Metropolitan police and the auxiliaries."

His eyes looked rheumy and his voice was choked as if he might break down at any moment.

She arranged the satchel bag around her body.

"Thank you, sir. You have risked your whole career and reputation for me. "

She extended a hand to him.

He took his hand in hers and placed his free one on top.

"It is all too little too late, and I am so sorry. I am sorry for turning my back on you for so long."

She met his gaze but could not find any words to express the huge well of emotion which was threatening to explode within her.

He released her hands and removed a leather wallet from his jacket pocket.

"Please, you must accept this. You will need a lot of money to reach London in these awful circumstances." A crisp five-pound note which showed the Kings profile lay in his palm.

She shook her head.

"No, It, was never about money sir."

"I know that, but you may need it, these are extraordinary times."

She hesitated while a pragmatic voice in her head reminded her that it was no time for displays of empty pride.

Sighing, she decided to accept it and raised her eyes to his as she mouthed.

"Thank you."

He remained silent but his expression told her everything. He was struggling under a similar weight as herself, a sense of sadness and happiness woven inextricably together.

At that moment she threw caution to the wind and stood on her toes as she reached for his cheek and planted a kiss on it. He smelled of antiseptic and tobacco smoke all in one.

He remained still, frozen like a statue except for the tears slipping down his face.

She whispered in his ear.

"Father – may I call thee Father you have just saved my life by your act of kindness."

The unexpected kiss overwhelmed him and for a few moments, he shook with emotion.

"I dare not call you daughter as I have not earned the right to do so but I wish you all the best."

His voice was almost imperceptible.

"I know." She smiled and then stepped away from him and headed for a small gate that led into a field of young oats.

Before opening it, she turned around to take one final look.

He was bent forward as if he carried the weight of the world on his shoulders. And the impenetrable mask of power had slipped.

She saw in his expression the bittersweet knowledge that he had lost out on all the joy that came with being her father.

He spoke in a shaky but loud voice.

"I want you to know that my marriage was an arranged one, I only met Esme one month before the wedding. When we set up home together and your lovely mother came to work for us, I was smitten. Once I heard that angelic voice, I fell in love with her. It transported me to other realms."

She said nothing but fixed her eyes upon his with an expression that seemed to move his soul. And he took several deep breaths as she spoke.

"It all makes sense to me now! Granny discouraged me from singing as a young girl even though my piano teacher was adamant that my voice should be trained."

He looked crestfallen as he replied.

"I am sorry to confirm that your grandmother believed it was her ethereal voice that placed her on the road to ruin."

Sarah nodded gravely.

If she started to comment on what he had just revealed it would be like releasing a dam. And so, she remained silent rather than release the string of angry words which were on the tip of her tongue.

Then she turned her back and released the rusty bolt. The gate opened with a series of squeaks and creaks.

"Farewell!" He called as she waved and went on her way.

At midday, she stopped for a long rest under the welcome shade of hedgerows while the sun beat down with ferocity. She was covered in sweat and decided to discard the corset she was wearing to hide her bump.

A small voice in her head admonished her.

No need to keep up appearances any longer - you have lost everything already.

She caressed her stomach for a few minutes before closing her eyes and falling asleep.

A couple of hours later, she awoke with a jolt and discovered that an army of ants was marching across her skirt. She jumped up and shook them off, amused at their military-like behaviour.

Her feet were sore and blistered but she had to continue with her journey.

By the time she reached the tinkers camp clouds were gathering.

She found the whole family, including several dogs and two piebald ponies under a cluster of ancient oaks. At some distance from them, a fire was crackling, and an old man sat gazing into the flames.

Despite her unkempt appearance, Biddy-Anne Ward recognised her immediately and hurried towards her.

"Miss, it's good to see you but I know that something is wrong"

Sarah nodded.

"Can we go somewhere and talk?"

Biddy-Anne eyed her suspiciously.

"I know you are in trouble, it's all over your face. Follow me."

They went deeper into the woods and stopped at a small clearing where a young man was polishing a brass harness.

"Kevin, get lost for a while, this woman wants to tell me something in private. And ask Tricksie to bring us mugs of hot tea and cold bacon with bread - I got some leftovers from the cook at that big red brick house this morning."

"Right," he said with a hang-dog expression as he sloped off.

They sat on the grass and Sarah decided to be brutally honest.

"I was attacked on Friday night last by Mel Geraghty in my own home - he intended to ravish me - and I killed him with the poker."

Biddy-Anne's mouth fell open to reveal a mouthful of black teeth.

"Do you mean that blackguard of a barber?"

Sarah nodded.

Biddy-Anne punched the air.

"He tried to put his yoke into me last year behind the church, but I gave him a kick in the hanging bits."

Sarah's face reddened.

"He has - I mean had no respect for women, I was terrified so I hit him again and again."

"I say it's a good riddance to bad rubbish!" Biddy-Anne blessed herself.

"They found his body in my cottage and are searching for me. I need to get into the city undercover, there is a house where I can hide."

Biddy-Anne's weather-beaten face looked at her.

"What do you want us to do?"

"I need to borrow a shawl and pretend to be married to one of your menfolk. I could travel in a wagon into the city centre if one of them agreed to drive me."

There was a silence and it seemed to Sarah like precious hours were ticking away while she waited for an answer.

A hedgehog scurried away into a ditch as a young bedraggled boy with a skinny dog ran after it.

"Frankie, leave it alone! We are busy," Biddy-Anne shouted.

The boy shrugged.

"But Pa likes roast hedgehog."

Biddy-Anne picked up a stick and threw it at him.

"Go away!"

Sarah could not tolerate the suspense any longer.

"Will you help me? I will swing at the end of a rope if they catch me!"

Biddy-Anne coughed.

"Yeah, we will help you. I could never forget the kindness you showed my boy, Bee. But just let me explain it to Big John, he is my uncle and the head of this camp."

Sarah's face softened.

"I have money which I can give you."

Biddy-Anne waved her hand in the air.

"Keep it, miss, you will need every penny for that little one in your belly. I told you weeks ago that you are in the family way."

Before Sarah could reply a girl emerged from among the trees with a basket of food.

Sarah ate the scraps of pig ravenously, washed down with lukewarm tea which reeked of woodsmoke, while Biddy-Anne hurried off to plan for the journey into the city.

In little more than thirty minutes, the red and blue wagon with Big John cracking the whip left the tinker's camp. It was pulled by a black cob horse called Darkie, with strong bones and a steady disposition.

Inside the wagon, Sarah crouched awkwardly, she was squeamish about bugs of any kind and suspected that the pile of old blankets under her knees were alive with flees.

To the inexperienced eye, she looked like a young tinker woman, dressed in a mottled skirt with a shabby blouse and plaid moth-eaten shawl. While her long curly hair normally lustrous and piled high on top of her head had been cut to her jawline by Biddy-Anne and then combed through with hair oil.

Biddy-Anne sat beside her along with her cousin's baby and her youngest daughter, a girl of three, known as Tilly.

"If the peelers or Tans stop us, I will give a pinch to the nipper and he will scream like a vixen mating. So, they will move us on without delay."

Biddy-Anne gave a conspiratorial laugh.

Sarah's face brightened. "You are such a loyal friend to me, Biddy-Anne."

"Tinkers never forget anyone who helped them," Biddy-Anne said.

There was no light inside the wagon apart from rays of pale sunlight which flooded through the half door at the front.

Now and again, she caught flashes of other vehicles drawn by ponies or donkeys. However, from her precarious position, for most of the journey, all she could see was the horse's rump and his long, thick tail swishing back and forth at flies.

His smell too pervaded the wagon, a curious mixture of sweat, hay, and dung. By the time they reached the first cobbled street on the outskirts of the city, he was moving at a fast trot, but Big John tightened the reins and he slowed to a steady pace.

At that moment, Big John shouted at the top of his voice in a language Sarah could not understand.

She guessed it was the one used by Tinkers called the Cant.

Biddy-Anne sat bolt upright.

"Get ready! There is a road-block up ahead."

Carefully, Biddy-Anne roused the sleeping infant who stretched and looked around him at the unfamiliar surroundings.

The wagon was drawing to a halt as Big John uttered a string of words in his own tongue.

Biddy-Anne interpreted it for Sarah.

"He is wishing that they all drown in the reeds of the river Liffey so that they never make it back to their families in England."

Biddy-Anne nodded, too distressed by what might happen when the wagon was searched, to worry about the tinker's curse.

Two constables of the Metropolitan police stepped forward on either side of the wagon while in a nearby doorway a British Army officer watched with his Lee Enfield rifle at the ready.

"Come out now you bunch of stinking tinkers! And stand there in a line!"

The constable on the right roared in a strong Dublin accent as he pointed at a spot in front of the soldier.

Sarah clambered out, with the baby boy pressed to her bosom while Biddy-Anne followed with young Tilly by the hand.

"Stop sucking that thumb or it will fall off!"

The constable mocked Tilly, who ran and hid behind her mother's skirt.

Sarah held her breath while Big John jumped down from his perch and doffed his cap at the soldier in the shadows.

"It's a grand evening," Big John remarked as he stood beside Biddy-Anne but his attempt at small talk fell on deaf ears.

"Where are you going at this hour?"

The second constable crossed in front of Blackie and stared into Big John's face.

"This is my Mrs and that is my niece Nelly. Poor Nelly's baby has not long to live so we are going to the church in Berkley Road, a nun called Sr. Dolores is meeting us there - she has a relic which is said to cure sick infants."

The tinker man said as he crossed himself piously three times.

Right on cue Biddy-Anne surreptitiously pinched the baby in the arm and he started to wail.

"There is nothing wrong with his lungs anyway!"

The constable remarked as he eyed Sarah who was rocking the baby gently in her arms.

"Now, do not move while we investigate this shithole that passes as a wagon."

Then he beckoned to his colleague who joined him in the search.

Biddy-Anne gave a surreptitious wink at Sarah who was trying hard to play the part of the distressed mother.

Suddenly, Blackie, sensing that something was wrong gave a loud whinny and rattled his harness which in turn shook the wagon. The younger of the two constables emerged.

"You," he said pointing at Big John. "Get over to that old nag and keep him quiet or I will have him shot."

"Yes, sir."

Sarah prayed hard while the minutes dragged by. When both constables finally appeared, they were both chortling.

"It is full of jiggery-pokery!" The one with the pock-marked face remarked.

His companion stared at Biddy-Anne.

"I found a box of tarot cards, a crystal ball, and something like a pendulum. Are you in league with the devil?"

She was quick to allay his suggestion.

"Mr I am a God-fearing woman like all tinkers but my family across the water were related to gipsies and I got some of their ways. It brings in a few shillings and helps us feed the young uns."

He harrumphed. "It's all hocus pocus to me."

Behind them, a long queue was building.

"Jack, that's enough let them go. They are just tinkers." The constable with the bad skin shouted.

The man named Jack gave Blackie a tap on the back.

"That's a sweet cob and all the feathering on the legs is striking. Now, hurry up and move, we have more important people to deal with."

While Big John took his position at the front the others piled into the wagon. Then Blackie took off with a toss of her head happy like his master to be his way.

Inside the wagon, Biddy-Anne was whispering in her own tongue to the infant who was back in her arms. While Sarah too relieved for words, lay back and listened to the rhythmic clip-clop of the horse's hooves as he picked up speed.

And all the time Tilly was singing softly to herself, "Clippety - Clippety-clop."

At the Mater hospital, Big John brought the horse and wagon to a halt.

Biddy-Anne embraced Sarah.

"This is as far as we can go, it's near Stoneybatter. Mind yourself and that young one in your belly."

Sarah conceded.

"Thank you for everything, Biddy-Anne. You must be a real fortune-teller or was it just a guess?"

Biddy-Anne laughed.

"It was neither, like I said, when you have seen as many kids being brought into the world as me, you learn to read the signs."

Sarah put two pound notes into her hand.

"Take them and get something nice for yourself and the kids."

Biddy-Anne's voice was thick as she said.

"The blessings of God on you."

It took another half an hour before she reached her destination. Although dusk was falling, drovers were leading herds of cattle along the streets to the cattle market in Prussia St. where they would be sold the following morning.

She was chased by a gang of marauding youths who shouted at her.

"Tinker, will you give us a ride for a penny?"

In her eagerness to reach Mulroy's safe house she had forgotten that she was still disguised as a tinker woman.

Outside St. Luke's church, a woman dressed in black with a large crucifix in her hands stopped her.

"Where are you going? These streets are full of wicked men who want to lead young women astray."

Sarah remained silent as she studied the big round face staring at her.

The woman smiled coyly.

"Come with me for some supper. My sister is waiting for me at the other end of the street. We try to save girls from iniquity."

"I am no prostitute! Go home and save your own soul! You are nothing but a do-gooder!"

Sarah features were red with frustration as she turned on her heel and ran away.

She heard the woman shouting after her.

"You tinkers are all the same, no manners and no gratitude. A good horsewhipping would bring you to your senses."

The door to No. 34 was painted in a sombre black but it boasted a freshly polished brass knocker and large knob.

Sarah gave three firm knocks and waited.

Within minutes it was opened by a tall, middle-aged woman, dressed in a mauve skirt and matching blouse. Her short hair was grey while her eyes and skin were pale. Sarah remembered her as Barbara Mulroy, who was active in the local Cuman Na mBan branch when she was living in the city.

The woman studied Sarah from head to toe.

"You are the third tinker woman to call today! The leftovers are all gone, I am running a boarding house here not a charity."

When she lowered her eyes, Sarah lifted her head and their eyes met. However, she withdrew her gaze and was about to close the door when Sarah spoke.

"I am no tinker woman! Take a closer look at me!"

The woman seemed startled as she peered from behind the door.

Sarah pulled back the shawl from her shoulders and piled her greasy hair on top of her head.

The woman gave her a sidelong glance and then exploded with laughter.

"Oh my God! I was expecting you, Sarah. Your name is all over the newspapers, but your disguise is so good!"

"Suffice it to say that it afforded a safe journey for me here!" Sarah replied, with a slight smile.

"You had better go around to the side and I will let you in that way. We don't want anyone saying that I allowed a tinker woman in through the front door, it will only arouse suspicion and put tongues wagging."

Sarah nodded. Suddenly, now that she was in safe hands, the adrenaline which her body had produced in response to the stress of the last few days seemed to have dried up. All she wanted to do was sleep in a comfortable bed without the fear of being discovered.

Later, following a meal and a hot bath Barbara showed her to a small room in the attic which she reserved for active members on the run.

The soft feather bed felt like heaven to her weary bones and she wallowed in it. A large smile spread across her face as she thought of the pet name which Sean called her when they were in bed.

La Belle Durmiente or Sleeping Beauty in English.

It was a phrase which he had picked up from his Spanish violin teacher, all those years ago in London. She wondered what the plural for Sleeping Beauties was in Spanish, now that she was carrying a tiny baby.

Then her eyelids closed, heavy with sleep, and she sank into blissful oblivion.

Chapter Nineteen

On the slippery deck of the mail boat, the figure of the nun stood out among the other passengers. Holding tightly to the rail, her black monastic scapular which covered her shoulders both front and back, flapped in the strong breeze. While her coarse serge tunic draping to the ground was damp at the edges.

On her head was a white cornette, reminiscent of medieval religious communities, along with a swirling veil, while around her neck a cross of silver on a black cord glistened in the light. The habit contained two sets of sleeves, the larger one to be folded up for work or folded down for ceremonial occasions. Underneath all the layers of her ill-fitting, homespun disguise, Sarah's body was itching all over.

The Mulroy sisters had acquired the nun's habit for her along with false papers to match because the mail boats between Hollyhead and Liverpool were swarming with British agents. She had opted to stay on deck while the RMS Munster edged its way through the slimy waters of Kingston port and out into the cold dark green depths of Dublin Bay, hoping that the fresh breeze and briny tang of the air would cool her body down.

To her right she saw Dalkey Island and on her left were Ireland's Eye and the Hill of Howth.

Out of the blue, she felt a tug at her cornette but she held it down with her right hand.

Then over the noise of the boat ploughing through a strong current, she heard a woman with an American accent shouting.

"Conrad, stop it. You must not pull at the nun's attire."

She turned quickly to see a heavy-set woman in her late forties rebuking a tall young boy with a vacant look in his eyes.

"I am so sorry Sister, Conrad is not the full shilling, I am accompanying him to London where his parents live. We just spent the last few months in Dublin with his uncle while they were in South Africa."

Sarah bowed graciously as she imagined a real nun might have done in similar circumstances.

"Would you mind blessing him with your crucifix? He nearly died in the womb as his mother had a protracted labour. It's like he is far away in another world - I am not a Roman Catholic, but his parents are."

Sarah could feel panic rising in the pit of her stomach while the baby seemed to take delight in kicking at the same time.

The familiar voice in her head whispered.

You are not so smug now.

A small crowd had already gathered out of curiosity and she feared that others might start asking for similar blessings.

Then an inner voice prompted her.

Pretend to be from an enclosed order of nuns who have taken a vow of silence.

Putting her finger to her lips she indicated that she was forbidden to speak.

"Oh My God! I understand! You have taken a lifetime vow of silence."

The woman crossed herself.

Sarah was so relieved that she nodded profusely. Then she held the crucifix over the head of the boy and made the sign of the cross, three times.

The woman tried to interpret it for the boy who seemed oblivious to his so-called blessing.

"Conrad, this kind Sister has blessed you in the name of The Father, The Son and The Holy Ghost."

Sarah felt like laughing at the incongruity of her situation, instead, she gave a saintly smile while the woman removed a sovereign from her purse and insisted on placing it in Sarah's hand.

"You must accept it and pass it on to your Mother Superior. I have heard that enclosed orders like yours depend on the generosity of the public. You are so busy praying for sinners and the whole of humanity."

Again, Sarah nodded and smiled shyly. If she refused to accept the donation it would only arouse suspicion.

She left her hand on the boy's head and mumbled a few words. Then she pointed in the direction of the stairs and made her way indoors to seek a place where she could remain unnoticed until the boat reached Hollyhead.

A young man gave up his seat for her. It was in a quiet corner, well away from idle passers-by. She sank back into the chair and closed her eyes, all the time fingering the rosary beads around her waist as if she were in deep prayer.

While the rhythm of the boat beat a pathway through the choppy waters, she replayed her time with the Mulroys whose generosity knew no bounds.

She had stayed with them for five full days and nights while she regained her strength. Both sisters had worked assiduously for women's rights and the Dublin branch of the Suffragettes. Sometimes, the IRA leaders stayed with them, including Sean, who had spent a night there just a few weeks before his disappearance.

They were known affectionately by everyone as Essie and Derry. And Sarah had confided in them about her marriage to Sean, her pregnancy, and her real father. It had been such a relief to share all her secrets with them.

They insisted that a discreet doctor who lived locally and often attended to men on the run, call on her. He had arrived with a black case and did a thorough examination. Everything seemed to his satisfaction until he listened to his Doppler stethoscope while it was placed against her stomach.

"I think that you may be having twins, but I cannot be sure. When you reach London, you must have further tests to confirm this possibility."

The news did not come as a total shock to her. She had known from the early weeks that her stomach seemed extra big and it was the reason why she had worn the corset to conceal it. For hours after his visit, she racked her brain but could not recall if Sean had mentioned any twins on his side of the family.

Suddenly, a voice beside her brought her back to the present.

"Apples, oranges, and chocolate."

She jumped with fright as she opened her eyes to see a hawker with a basket of her wares under her nose.

She pointed at a bar of Fry's chocolate and removed a threepenny piece from her purse which she handed to the hawker.

"There you are, Sister."

The woman spoke with a pronounced Mayo accent as she placed the bar in Sarah's hand. "Will you say a prayer for me and my poor kids? I have a sick husband at home in Liverpool."

Sarah noticed that a tall, ruddy-faced man wearing a Mackintosh, just a few feet away, was listening intently.

She nodded and pulled out a Holy picture which she had found in the pocket of her habit.

Without uttering a word, she placed it in the hawker's hand and smiled.

"Thanks, so much, Sister." The woman said as she bowed her head out of respect.

The man who had by then lit a cigarette addressed the hawker in a half-Scottish accent.

"I am watching you! And if I find evidence that you are doing a bit of pick-pocketing on the side then I will cart you off to jail once this boat docks."

The hawker looked sideways at him and then protested her innocence loudly as she hurried upstairs to the upper deck.

Sarah closed her eyes and sighed, resuming her prayerful pose while he moved off to watch other passengers. For one awful moment, she had been convinced that he was watching her. She went back to her own thoughts, nibbling discreetly at the black chocolate every now and then when no one was passing. If she really had twins in her womb, she knew it would require a miracle of sorts for her to deliver even one healthy baby safely, after all she had put her body through in recent weeks.

The Mulroy sisters had sent a telegram to Maddie in London, informing her of Sarah's imminent arrival and she could hardly wait to be safely ensconced in her friend's flat near Chiswick. She had also posted a brief letter to Rita in Belfast, outlining what had happened and reassuring her that she was on her way to London. Sooner or later Rita would read about Geraghty's murder in back-dated copies of the Meath Chronicle from some newsagent in Belfast, and it was better that she heard about the murder from Sarah's own hand. Nervously, Sarah rearranged the double sleeves of her habit. She could not wipe the image of

William Taylor from her mind. She had wasted so much energy on hating him.

A tiny interior voice reminded her.

And now, I must sooner or later come to terms with the fact that he is my real father.

Once she settled in London, she would commit to paper the torrent of mixed feelings which she had about him. In her teen years, writing in her diary had been a form of cathartic release for her.

Then, a faint, invidious voice inside her asked;

Will you write to him?

Surely, you owe him that much?

While in her belly she felt flutter like movements, reminding her that she had much more pressing issues to deal with.

The Mulroys had promised to contact her immediately if there was any news about Sean.

She had so much to tell him that sometimes without warning she wept from sheer frustration. And most of all she longed to tell him that she was pregnant with at least one if not two of his babies. Only the previous night she had dreamt that they were strolling together on the hill of Tara where he was shouting with joy to the four winds about her pregnancy.

Even now, she had no regrets about one minute of her time with him.

She had understood when she married him that he was 'a wanted man' and that he lived his life dangerously. Fear of him being caught and executed was the reason for her insisting that they get married in a secret ceremony in London rather than wait for peacetime, as she wanted to make the most of every day.

She crossed herself and uttered a silent prayer.

She was slowly starting to acknowledge that even retrieving his body would be better than the present limbo in which she found herself.

She recalled women whose husbands had enlisted with The Royal Dublin Fusiliers and never returned from the Great War. They had told her that the dreaded abbreviation; MIA (Missing in action on official correspondence) was far worse than having his body returned to them. The thought of never being wrapped in his arms again filled her body with shock and her hands shook violently, underneath the folds of her coarse sleeves.

Slowly, she started to count to one hundred in her head, she must not draw any more attention upon herself.

Two hours later.

"Hurry! We are just passing the South Stack Lighthouse at the western point of Holyhead Island!"

A man rushed down the steps from above and shouted to his wife and children.

Sarah scratched her arms discreetly. How she longed to be rid of her nun's garb.

Once they docked, all that stood between her and freedom was the train journey to London.

There, assuming her new identity as a young widow woman, with papers to match, she would be safe.

She went up onto the deck where large groups of passengers were waiting, as the boat inched through the busy port and the tedious business of docking began.

The cold salty air filled her lungs and she relaxed when she saw the twinkling lights of the tiny Welsh town.

Nearby, an old woman with a strong Galway accent remarked to her teenage granddaughter.

"Maybe you should consider joining a convent."

The young girl retorted.

"Granny you are so old-fashioned, I don't want to spend my life flagellating myself in some cloistered abbey. The suffragists have already achieved votes for older women and soon we will all have the vote."

Sarah heard the conversation just before the wind whipped it out to sea. And she was so grateful about her impending freedom that she laughed out loud like a giddy schoolgirl.

The old woman turned to study her.

"Imagine a nun making a show of herself in public! In my day, a nun would not be permitted to travel alone."

Her granddaughter had the final word.

"Granny, this is the twentieth century! Times are changing."

Chapter Twenty

Six weeks later, after endless nights of broken sleep punctuated by nightmares, Sarah had to admit that she needed professional help. She was staying with Maddie in a pretty two bedroomed cottage near Ealing, on the west side of London. She would never forget Maddie's kindness and non-judgemental attitude from the moment she turned up on her doorstep. Ealing while still, a rural area was within easy reach of the metropolis. She had assumed the name of Annie Maloney and had papers to match thanks to the Mulroy sisters and friends of Sean who lived among the Irish community in Cricklewood. She had also had an appointment with an obstetrician who confirmed that she was carrying twins, but he had picked up on the fact that she was in a high state of anxiety.

Fearful of disclosing that she was a fugitive from British justice in Ireland, she laid all the blame for her troubled state on the premature death of her mother and the absence of a father figure. He recommended that she seek psychoanalysis before the arrival of her babies complicated things even further.

With no money to spare she sought the assistance of Sean's brother, Fr. Shay who was the Parish Priest in a wealthy location known as Ribisbury-on-Thames. His generosity knew no bounds and he had arranged for her to have sessions with a specialist from the Institute of Psychoanalysis.

And so, it happened that at noon on midsummer's day she found herself slowly taking the last few steps up to the red door with the highly polished knocker and matching knob. With a heavy heart, she paused and took several deep breaths while she studied the brass plate on the wall which proclaimed: DR Richard Hunter.

Then she pressed the knocker and waited while it echoed through the house. Eventually, after what seemed like an hour, a middle-aged woman with a neat grey bun and dull brown suit opened the door.

Sarah swallowed hard. "I have an appointment …"

The secretary looked her up and down disdainfully.

"Mrs Maloney I presume, do follow me I shall show you into the doctor's surgery. I believe he is on the telephone right now."

She took off at a fast pace through a long, dimly lit entrance hall while Sarah hurried to keep up with her. After a few minutes, the secretary paused outside a white door and opened it slowly.

"Take a seat or if you prefer lie on the couch, in other words, do whatever it takes to make you relax."

The secretary glanced suspiciously at Sarah and then she turned her back and disappeared into a small office with the door ajar.

Sighing, Sarah entered the room cautiously, unsure if she should leave the door open. On the spur of the moment, she closed it and studied her surroundings. The room was large with three long Georgian windows and high ceilings covered in ornate plasterwork. A mahogany desk with two high backed chairs on either side took pride of place in the centre of the room while matching bookcases stuffed with scholarly journals and heavy medical tomes were arranged along the walls. To the right of the empty fireplace, her eye fell on a couch draped with two tartan rugs.

Suddenly, the door opened and a heavy-set man in his late sixties burst into the room.

He chuckled to himself as he moved towards his desk with head bent. For a moment Sarah wondered if he had seen her at all. She cleared her throat.

"Excuse me, but your secretary told me to wait here."

He nodded.

"Take a seat, I must locate my fountain pen and some paper."

She sat on the edge of the chair while he rummaged in a drawer until he found a stout black pen and a leather-bound notebook. Then much to her relief he extended a hand to her and declared.

"Please call me Richard, I shall call you Sarah. I want to dispense with formalities because I need you to feel safe and comfortable with me so that we can improve your mental well-being and help you have a happy and fulfilled life."

She smiled as she felt his warm, reassuring handshake. "Thank you, Richard."

"Now, my dear lady, allow me to tell you a little about myself. I studied under Sigmund Freud, but that is not to say that I do everything his way. I take it you are aware of his work."

"Indeed, I am." She allowed her body to settle back into the chair.

"Good. You see I have refined many of his ideas after a lifetime of working in this field. Your dear brother-in-law Fr. Byrne has confided in me about recent happening in your life. So, I want to assure you that your secrets are all safe with me. I am only interested in making you whole again. My own mother was American but had Irish roots, which means I feel an affinity with the Irish people."

She wiped a tear from her eye.

"Thank you so much, it is good to be reassured that our sessions will be strictly confidential. I have much to get off my chest. Where should I begin?"

He lit a fat cigar while she waited for an answer. Then when he had taken a puff from it, he replied.

"Begin where you wish, last month last year or even in your childhood. It's all the same to me, I need to make sure that you fully trust me before our real work begins."

For a few seconds, she studied his kind, intelligent eyes and deeply furrowed brow and knew that she could trust him implicitly.

"I want to start with my husband's disappearance." Her hands shook but she continued. "And the fact that I ended up killing a man who was trying to -."

Words failed her, but he responded in a soothing voice.

"Take your time my dear lady, we have all the time in the world."

He doodled in his notepad.

"And to add insult to injury the man I believed to be my arch enemy has turned out to be my real father and I feel so confused about him."

Without any warning, she began to sob uncontrollably while he sat back in his chair and looked out the window. When it seemed to her that she had cried an ocean of tears but still could not stop, he began to blow hideous shapes from his cigar smoke. To her astonishment, she felt her tears give way to laughter and she wondered if she was about to descend into madness.

However, she could hear his voice reassuring her.

"Don't worry tears, and laughter are just different sides of the same coin, they are outward responses to trauma, fear, and exhaustion."

She nodded gratefully and then sipped at the glass of water which he placed in front of her.

Slowly, while the gold clock on the mantelpiece ticked away the minutes, she blurted out all about Sean's disappearance and then the details of how she had ended up taking a man's life. And as she unburdened herself of her deepest thoughts and feelings, she realised that there was a light at the end of the tunnel and that in due course this man would help her reach it.

Later, that evening she strolled along a towpath on the banks of the Thames with Maddie and Fr. Shay.

"The world and his wife are here, enjoying this glorious sunshine. It's hard to believe that it's almost eight pm," Fr. Shay remarked as he wiped his forehead with a handkerchief.

Maddie, forever the joker, remarked, "Look at you, sweating like a pig. Would the bishop mind if just for one evening you took off all that heavy black clothing and walked around in regular, summer clothes?"

He threw back his head and guffawed.

"Do you want to have me excommunicated by the Pope?"

With a twinkle in her eye, Maddie answered.

"Would that really matter in the grand scheme of things?"

Sarah looked from her friend to her brother-in-law and then giggled like a schoolgirl. For the first time in months, she felt able to live in the moment and enjoy the company of those around her.

Suddenly, she got a delicious smell as a young couple passed them by eating chips and battered cod from greasy brown papers interspersed with old newspapers.

"Hurry up! Let's turn back, I saw a fish and chip shop earlier when we got off the train and I say we treat ourselves to some!"

Maddie and Fr. Shay exchanged glances of utter relief. They both felt reassured now that Sarah, would in due course recover from her recent traumas, and that she would be well able to meet the challenges of being a sole parent to twins.

"What about my poor figure?" Maddie teased her friend.

Sarah, who was at the head of the group shouted back in a jocular fashion.

"Don't know, don't care! I can eat what I like as I am eating for three!"

Then she began to hum a song called "The Foggy Dew", within seconds the others joined her in the chorus while they followed a winding path that led to the pretty village of Hillham.

Epilogue

1930

At 3:20 in the afternoon, on a hot August day, Sarah found it hard to concentrate on the ceremony which was about to take place. It was not just the blistering heat but the fact that since the killing of Mel Geraghty, this was just her second time back on Irish soil. She had only managed to pluck up the courage for one brief visit to Rita in Belfast.

Much had changed since her perilous journey disguised as a nun on the mail boat from Dun Laoghaire to Hollyhead ten years earlier when, she had escaped with her life from the idiosyncrasies of British justice. Ireland was now known as the Irish Free State, independent from the United Kingdom, with its own government led by W.T Cosgrave, but still within the British Empire. However, if she remained in the country sooner or later, she would have to face the full rigor of the law in a society where there was no gender justice. And swing at the end of a rope or spend the rest of her life incarcerated in a lunatic asylum.

Yet she was content with the new life that she had carefully built for herself and her children in London. And she was making a real change to the daily lives of the poor Irish immigrants in Camden Town, working by day as a teacher and in the evenings on a voluntary basis with groups of semi- literate men and women. Her years teaching in the most deprived parts of that great city had not gone unnoticed and she had even earned a prestigious award, albeit under her assumed name, from the local community.

Now with a broad smile, from her place of honour in the front row of chairs she took a few moments to study her surroundings. The village green in the centre of Brachnew, Co. Cork was bedecked with green white and gold bunting while a tricolour to match flew proudly from a pole in the very centre. Nearby the leaves of a young oak tree (in a large wooden tub) wilted in the blazing sunshine as if to protest at the long wait before being transplanted into the fertile space prepared for it.

While on the ground in front, a small stone memorial concealed by scarlet velvet would soon be unveiled. It bore the following inscription:

In memory of Sean Byrne,
now playing second fiddle to the angels.
Born in this parish in 1886,
a brave and talented Irishman.
He fought in the 1916 Rising,
and in the guerrilla war that followed,
until his untimely death in 1920.

When the seats behind her began to fill up Sarah cast a glance back at the rows of faces, some familiar and some unfamiliar.

The Mulroy sisters chatting to their famous brothers. Fr. Byrne, Sean's brother with a group of his relatives. Eamonn Geraghty whispering sweet nothings into his fiancé's ear. Rosie Mc Ginley, now widowed, with Bee and his gypsy wife Silvia from Bucharest. Finally, a group of comrades, friends and acquaintances who had fought alongside Sean.

While to her left, seated in her row were her identical twin daughters Niamh and Maeve giggling among themselves. Next came Rita who was keeping a close eye on the two freckled faced girls. And finally, Maddie who looked more glamorous than ever in a wide brimmed hat with matching green dress. However, one space remained empty in the end of that line of chairs.

Sarah checked the time nervously.

In a matter of minutes, the ceremony would begin.

She hoped and prayed that her final guest would come, in the end it was his decision. Her mind recalled her arrival in London, there she had plenty of time to reflect on the murder which she had committed in Ireland. And slowly she learned that she was in no position to judge anyone even her real father, and so she put pen to paper and wrote to him.

Initially, the letters which went back and forth between them were taut. Then as the months turned into years he asked more and more about his grandchildren until he eventually travelled to London to see them. During that month there was a seismic change in the father- daughter relationship, when he established a good rapport with the girls who were just two years old. She decided then that it was not fair to deprive them of knowing their only living grandparent given that they had also lost their father. And in a curious twist, she discovered as the years unfolded that forgiveness bestows more on the giver than the receiver.

The ceremony had been rehearsed earlier with the President of the local committee.

A lone piper would begin with a lament. Followed by short speeches from Fr. Byrne and John Monaghan, a life-long friend of Sean`s. Then, while a local fiddler played a medley of Sean`s favourite music, she would be invited to plant the young oak in its new position at the centre of the green.

Finally, the twins would unveil the memorial to their late father.

Just as the piper was about to sound the first note, she noticed a member of the committee signalling that he should hold off. From the corner of her eye, she saw a thin, frail man on crutches being supported by a nurse. Her heart almost burst with happiness.

The twins, much to Rita`s dissatisfaction pointed excit-edly in his direction. And Maeve, the most outgoing of the pair, overjoyed to see her grandfather called.

"Grandad, we are over here!"

He lifted a bony hand and waved to her while his rheumy eyes filled with tears.

The Right, Honourable William Taylor, retired Resident Magistrate, and the man she had come, albeit slowly, to know and accept as her father had arrived despite his ongoing battle with cancer, to support her on this the hardest of days.

An important day when she would formerly acknowledge along with his relatives and friends that Sean was never coming home. The ceremony would not only commemorate the man and the soldier but would ring fence the fact that his disappearance would remain a mystery forever. For years, false sightings of him in Belfast, London, New York and even Canada had trickled back to her. Each time she would hope against all hope and then it would end in heart- wrenching disappointment.

Without a body and without a funeral there was no ending.

This ceremony would bring closure for everyone but most of all for herself and her beloved twins. She had cherished memories of the short time she had shared with Sean. And every day she would be reminded of him because the girls had the same sparkling blue eyes.

A huge tear slipped down her left cheek and she wiped it hurriedly away, hoping that no one had noticed.

Then, along with the assembled crowd she stood to attention when the sound of the Uilleann Pipes filled the air. And just as the last notes of Danny Boy faded, a pair of swans flew directly overhead. All eyes turned skywards to follow the course of the birds who were heading for the nearby lake with a series of hissing and grunting noises, their wings making a haunting, primeval sound. Emotion welled up inside Sarah and this time she made no effort to hide her tears because they were tears of joy. Sean had spoken so often about the majesty of the swans that he had encountered along the banks of the Boyne as he crept from one secret location to another. Now, she knew instinctively that he had sent them as messengers to reassure her that he was at peace.

The End

About the Author

Anne Frehill has had short stories and non -fiction published in a range of magazines.

She has also contributed to Sunday Miscellany on RTE Radio 1, and was included in a book relating to the same programme, edited by Marie Heaney comprising the best writing from 2003 and 2004. Since the start of the Pandemic, she has written regularly in a local online newsletter, on a range of topics.

Anne has an abiding interest in history, folklore, sociology and nature. And is passionate about animal welfare and care of the earth. She lives in Meath in the heart of farming country.

Please Review

Dear Reader,

If you enjoyed this book, would you kindly post a short review on Amazon? Your feedback will make all the difference to getting the word out about this book.

To leave a review, go to Amazon and type in the book title. When you have found it go to the book page, please scroll to the bottom of the page to where it says 'Write a Review' and then submit your review.

Thank you in advance.

13.05 Rowpolus

Euns

12.75 W.S.H.

9 781914 225215